LITERATURE MADE EASY

THOMAS HARDY'S

FAR from the
MADDING
CROWD

Written by STEVE EDDY
WITH TONY BUZAN

BARRON'S

First edition for the United States and Canada published by Barron's
Educational Series, Inc., 1999.

Copyright © 1999 U.S. version, Barron's Educational Series, Inc.

First published in the United Kingdom by Hodder & Stoughton Ltd.
under the title: *Teach Yourself Literature Guides: A Guide to Far
from the Madding Crowd*

Copyright © 1997 Steve Eddy
Introduction Copyright © 1997 Tony Buzan

Cover photograph © The Ronald Grant Archive
Mind Maps: David Creasey
Illustrations: Karen Donnelly

Steve Eddy asserts the moral right to be identified as the
author of this work.

American text edited by Benjamin Griffith.

All inquiries should be addressed to:
Barron's Educational Series, Inc.
250 Wireless Boulevard
Hauppauge, New York 11788
http://www.barronseduc.com

International Standard Book No. 0-7641-0824-7

Library of Congress Catalog Card No. 98-74379

Printed in the United States of America
9 8 7 6 5 4 3 2 1

CONTENTS

How to study	iv
How to use this guide	viii
Key to icons	ix
Background	1
The story of *Far from the Madding Crowd*	3
Who's who?	6
• Gabriel Oak: Steady young farmer	6
• Sergeant Troy: Soldier and womanizer	8
• Boldwood: Middle-aged gentleman farmer	10
• Bathsheba: Farmer and local love goddess	11
• Fanny Robin: A tragic victim	13
• Liddy: Bathsheba's gossipy maid-companion	13
• The rustics: Bathsheba's workers	14
Themes	16
• Love	16
• Loyalty	18
• Men and women	18
• Nature	20
• Time and change	21
• The Church and blind chance	22
• Craft	23
Commentary	25
Topics for discussion and brainstorming	77
How to get an "A" in English Literature	78
The exam essay	79
Model answer and essay plan	80
Glossary of literary terms	84
Index	85

There are five important things you must know about your brain and memory to revolutionize
the way you study:

◆ how your memory
  ("recall") works *while* you are learning
◆ how your memory works *after* you have finished learning
◆ how to use Mind Maps – a special technique for helping you
  with all aspects of your studies
◆ how to increase your reading speed
◆ how to prepare for tests and exams

Recall during learning
– THE NEED FOR BREAKS

When you are studying, your memory
can concentrate, understand, and
remember well for between 20 and 45
minutes at a time, then it needs a break.
If you continue for longer than this
without a break, your memory starts to
break down. If you study for hours nonstop, you will remember
only a small fraction of what you have been trying to learn, and
you will have wasted hours of valuable time.

So, ideally, *study for less than an hour*, then take a five- to ten-
minute break. During the break listen to music, go for a walk, do
some exercise, or just daydream. (Daydreaming is a necessary
brain-power booster – geniuses do it regularly.) During the break
your brain will be sorting out what it has been learning, and you
will go back to your books with the new information safely
stored and organized in your memory. We recommend breaks
at regular intervals as you work through the Literature Guides.
Make sure you take them!

Recall after learning
– THE WAVES OF YOUR MEMORY

What do you think begins to happen to your memory right after you have finished learning something? Does it immediately start forgetting? No! Your brain actually *increases* its power and continues remembering. For a short time after your study session, your brain integrates the information, making a more complete picture of everything it has just learned. Only then does the rapid decline in memory begin, and as much as 80 percent of what you have learned can be forgotten in a day.

However, if you catch the top of the wave of your memory, and briefly review (look back over) what you have been studying, the memory is imprinted far more strongly, and stays at the crest of the wave for a much longer time. To maximize your brain's power to remember, take a few minutes at the end of a day and use a Mind Map to review what you have learned. Then review it at the end of a week, again at the end of a month, and finally a week before your test or exam. That way you'll ride your memory wave all the way there – and beyond!

The Mind Map®
– A PICTURE OF THE WAY YOU THINK

Do you like taking notes? More important, do you like having to go back over and learn them before tests or exams? Most students I know certainly do not! And how do you take your notes? Most people take notes on lined paper, using blue or black ink. The result, visually, is boring. And what does *your* brain do when it is bored? It turns off, tunes out, and goes to sleep! Add a dash of color, rhythm, imagination, and the whole note-taking process becomes much more fun, uses more of your brain's abilities, and improves your recall and understanding.

Generally, your Mind Map is highly personal and need not be understandable to any other person. It mirrors *your* brain. Its purpose is to build up your "memory muscle" by creating images that will help you recall instantly the most important points about characters and plot sequences in a work of fiction you are studying.

You will find Mind Maps throughout this book. Study them, add some color, personalize them, and then try drawing your own—you'll remember them far better. Stick them in your files and on your walls for a quick-and-easy review of the topic.

HOW TO DRAW A MIND MAP

1 First of all, briefly examine the Mind Maps and Mini Mind Maps used in this book. What are the common characteristics? All of them use small pictures or symbols, with words branching out from the illustration.
2 Decide which idea or character in the book you want to illustrate and then draw a picture, starting in the middle of the page so that you have plenty of room to branch out. Remember that no one expects a young Rembrandt or Picasso here; artistic ability is not as important as creating an image that you (and you alone) will remember. A round smiling (or sad) face might work as well in your memory as a finished portrait. Use marking pens of different colors to make your Mind Map as vivid and memorable as possible.
3 As your thoughts flow freely, add descriptive words and other ideas that connect to the central image. Print clearly, using one word per line if possible.
4 Further refine your thinking by adding smaller branching lines, containing less important facts and ideas, to the main points.
5 Presto! You have a personal outline of your thoughts and concepts about the characters and plot. It's not a stodgy formal outline, but a colorful image that will stick in your mind, it is hoped, throughout classroom discussions and final exams.

HOW TO READ A MIND MAP

1 Begin in the center, the focus of your topic.
2 The words/images attached to the center are like chapter headings; read them next.
3 Always read out from the center, in every direction (even on the left-hand side, where you will have to read from right to left, instead of the usual left to right).

USING MIND MAPS

Mind Maps are a versatile tool; use them for taking notes in class or from books, for solving problems, for brainstorming with friends, and for reviewing and working for tests or exams–their uses are endless. You will find them invaluable for planning essays for coursework and exams. Number your main branches in the order in which you want to use them and off you go – the main headings for your essay are done and all your ideas are logically organized!

Preparing for tests and exams

◆ Review your work systematically. Study hard at the beginning of the course, not the end, and avoid "exam panic!"
◆ Use Mind Maps throughout your course, and build a Master Mind Map for each subject, a giant Mind Map that summarizes everything you know about the subject.
◆ Use memory techniques such as mnemonics (verses or systems for remembering things like dates and events).
◆ Get together with one or two friends to study, compare Mind Maps, and discuss topics.

AND FINALLY...

Have *fun* while you learn – it has been shown that students who make their studies enjoyable understand and remember everything better and get the highest grades. I wish you and your brain every success!

(Tony Buzan)

HOW TO USE THIS GUIDE

This guide assumes that you have already read *Far from the Madding Crowd*, although you could read Background and The Story of *Far from the Madding Crowd* before that. It is best to use the guide alongside the novel. You could read the Who's Who? and Themes sections without referring to the novel, but you will get more out of these sections if you do refer to it, especially when thinking about the questions designed to test your recall and help you think about the novel.

The Commentary section can be used in a number of ways. One way is to read a chapter or part of a chapter in the novel, and then read the Commentary for that section. Continue until you come to a test section, test yourself, and then take a break. Or, read the Commentary for a chapter, then read that chapter in the novel, then go back to the Commentary.

Topics for Discussion and Brainstorming gives topics that could well appear on exams or provide a basis for coursework. It would be particularly useful for you to discuss them with friends, or brainstorm them using Mind Map techniques (see p. vi).

How to Get an "A" in English Literature gives valuable advice on what to look for in a text, and what skills you need to develop in order to achieve your personal best.

The Exam Essay is a useful night-before reminder of how to tackle exam questions, and Model Answer and Essay Plan gives an example of an "A"-grade essay and the Mind Map and plan used to write it.

The questions

Whenever you come across a question in the guide with a star ✪ in front of it, think about it for a moment. You could even jot down a few words to focus your mind. There is not usually a "right" answer to these questions; it is important for you to develop your own opinions if you want to get an "A." The Test Yourself sections are designed to take you about 10–20 minutes each. Take a short break after each one.

Themes

A **theme** is an idea explored by an author. Whenever a theme is dealt with in the guide, the appropriate icon is used. This means you can find where a theme is mentioned just by leafing through the book. Go on – try it now!

Love

Time and change

Loyalty

Fate

Men and women

Craft

Nature

✍ STYLE AND LANGUAGE

This heading and icon are used in the Commentary wherever there is a special section on the author's choice of words and imagery.

One of the most important elements in this novel is the richness of the imagery with which Hardy, who was a poet as well as a novelist, describes nature. Literary critics write of his descriptions as "landscapes with figures," and often the sights and sounds of nature convey to the reader the somber, foreboding atmosphere Hardy intends as the background of the action. Make notes of the lines that particularly appeal to you.

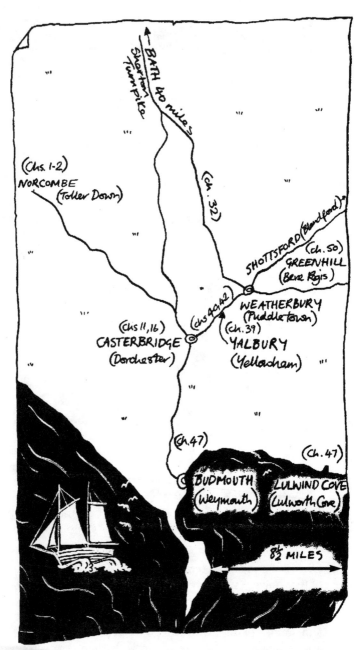

The Weatherbury area. What happens where?

BACKGROUND

Hardy was born in rural Dorset in 1840, three years after Queen Victoria came to the throne. His father was a builder and stonemason, his mother a former servant. He left school at 16 to pursue a career in architecture, but the success of *Far from the Madding Crowd*, when he was 34, enabled him to become a full-time writer.

Country life versus city life

Hardy, who grew up in rural western England, showed his dislike for cities in the novel's title, and the "madding" crowd (which comes from poet Thomas Gray's line, "Far from the madding crowd's ignoble strife") was indeed maddening to him. He preferred the countryside, where he could experience closely the changing rhythms of the seasons throughout the farming year, as well as the customs and speech of the simple rural people. The setting provides a resonant and realistic background to the dramatic actions of his principal characters.

Part of the reason for the novel's instant popularity was that it reflected a widespread longing. Hardy was writing at a time of rapid industrialization. Cities were growing fast. Many readers longed for what they imagined was the idyllic, timeless world of the countryside, though even the countryside itself was now changing, as railroads cut through it and agricultural machinery began to put farm laborers out of work.

Far from the Madding Crowd is set in a golden age of agriculture, during the 1840s. There is little movement of families to or from Weatherbury, so there is a strong sense of continuing community. As a result, small weaknesses – such as Joseph's nervousness – are accepted. Even minor villains like Pennyways are generously tolerated. Trouble seems to come only with the arrival of newcomers, like Bathsheba and Troy.

Despite the general sense of harmony, life is not easy. Working hours are long, and holidays limited to a few annual festival days, so minor illness is seen as a rare chance to read a book or learn a card game (see Chapter 33). There is little opportunity for personal advancement, though a brave individual might emigrate, as Gabriel plans to do. Troy does go to America, but fails to make a real success of it.

Poverty is a constant threat. Even Gabriel cannot count on finding work when forced to present himself at a hiring fair. The one straw at which the destitute can clutch is the Poor Law: Someone who has been employed within a parish for a year can claim the bare minimum of food and shelter in a workhouse, like the one in which Fanny dies.

A *military life*

One area of employment in which a man could advance himself was the army. Here, food and shelter were guaranteed, along with a dashing red uniform that had a powerful romantic appeal to young women, and enough spending money to ensure that publicans and prostitutes would always welcome a new regiment's arrival. The disadvantage was the risk of being sent abroad on active service.

P*ublication*

Like many novels, *Far from the Madding Crowd* was first published in serial form in the *Cornhill* magazine. This is partly why the novel falls easily into separate episodes and why some chapters end with something dramatic that leaves the reader eager for more. Look at the chapter endings to see this for yourself.

This form of publication also meant that Hardy had to be aware of the moral outlook of his readers. The magazine's editor, Leslie Stephen, warned Hardy that he would have to deal with Troy's seduction of Fanny "in a very gingerly fashion." Be aware of this as you read; see if there is anything that would shock your grandparents!

THE STORY OF *FAR FROM THE MADDING CROWD*

Gabriel Oak, a young farmer, encounters newcomer Bathsheba Everdene, who is beautiful but vain. He watches her, and on one occasion she saves his life. He tries to court her, but she refuses him.

Bathsheba inherits a farm in Weatherbury. Gabriel is ruined when most of his sheep die. On his way to look for work, he helps to fight a haystack fire, and is hired by the owner, Bathsheba. Soon, Bathsheba fires her thieving manager, Pennyways, and runs the farm herself. It comes out that her servant Fanny has run off with a soldier.

A THOUGHTLESS PRANK

Bathsheba sends serious-minded Farmer Boldwood a valentine as a joke. He discovers that it is from her. Fanny's soldier, Troy, waits in church to marry her, but she arrives too late and Troy leaves in a rage.

Boldwood falls in love with Bathsheba and proposes. Undecided, she consults Gabriel and then fires him for giving his opinion. However, she has to swallow her pride when her sheep are in danger of dying. Gabriel saves them and stays on.

A DASHING STRANGER

One night, Bathsheba meets a flirtatious stranger, Troy, when her dress catches on his spur. He gradually wins her with charm, flattery, and swordplay. She tries to fire Gabriel again when he warns her against her new lover.

She writes a letter to Boldwood, rejecting him. He begs for her pity and vows revenge on Troy. Bathsheba rides at night to Bath and returns married to Troy, who at first conceals this from Boldwood in order to taunt him. When the truth emerges, Boldwood despairs. At the harvest supper, Troy gets the men drunk, and Gabriel, helped by Bathsheba, has to work all night to save the grain from a storm.

Troy gambles his money away. He and Bathsheba meet the now pregnant Fanny on the road, but Bathsheba does not recognize her. Fanny struggles to get to Casterbridge, where she and her baby die. Troy admits that a lock of hair that Bathsheba finds belongs to his former fiancée, the woman on the road. News of Fanny's death arrives. Joseph Poorgrass goes to get her body but gets drunk coming back. The funeral delayed, the coffin is brought into Bathsheba's house for the night. Tormented by suspicion, Bathsheba opens it and finds the dead baby. Troy enters, kisses Fanny, and rejects Bathsheba. He buys Fanny an expensive gravestone and plants flowers on her grave.

TROY LEAVES WEATHERBURY

When Troy discovers that a spouting gargoyle has spoiled Fanny's grave, he despairs, and leaves Weatherbury. Arriving at the sea, he is saved from drowning by a passing boat. Bathsheba hears that he is dead. She is unconvinced, but eventually thinks it may be true. Gabriel becomes estate manager for both Bathsheba and Boldwood. Boldwood's hopes are renewed.

Months later, Troy is in a traveling show that he has joined on returning from America. Bathsheba sees the show, but he manages to conceal his identity. Boldwood urges Bathsheba to promise to marry him after waiting the required six years time.

BOLDWOOD'S DESPAIR

Boldwood holds a Christmas party at which he extracts the promise from Bathsheba, but at that point Troy appears and claims her back. In a fit of passion, Boldwood shoots Troy and kills him. He is sentenced to hang, but then given life imprisonment instead on grounds of mental instability. Some months later, Gabriel gives Bathsheba his notice. She visits him and hints that she might marry him if asked. They marry – to the approval of all the workers.

before finding out who's who, brush up on the plot by looking at the flowchart opposite

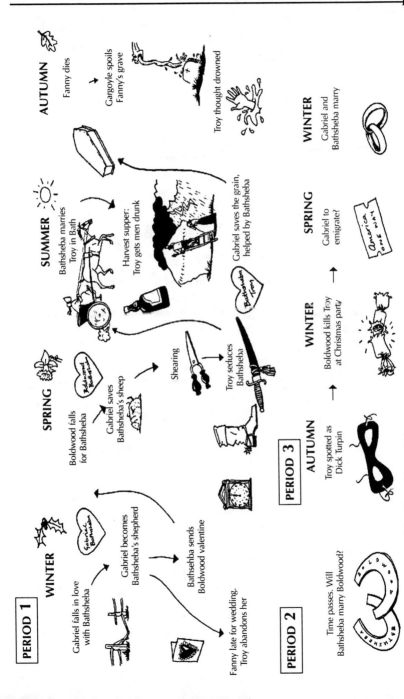

PERIOD 1

WINTER

Gabriel falls in love with Bathsheba

Gabriel becomes Bathsheba's shepherd

Bathsheba sends Boldwood valentine

Fanny late for wedding. Troy abandons her

SPRING

Boldwood falls for Bathsheba

Gabriel saves Bathsheba's sheep

Shearing

Troy seduces Bathsheba

SUMMER

Bathsheba marries Troy in Bath

Harvest supper: Troy gets men drunk

Gabriel saves the grain, helped by Bathsheba

AUTUMN

Fanny dies

Troy thought drowned

Gargoyle spoils Fanny's grave

PERIOD 2

Time passes. Will Bathsheba marry Boldwood?

PERIOD 3

AUTUMN

Troy spotted as Dick Turpin

WINTER

Boldwood kills Troy at Christmas party

SPRING

Gabriel to emigrate?

America ONE WAY

WINTER

Gabriel and Bathsheba marry

The story of *Far from the Madding Crowd* through the seasons

WHO'S WHO?

The Mini Mind Map above summarizes the characters in *Far from the Madding Crowd*. Test yourself by looking at the full Mind Map on p. 15 and then copying the Mini Mind Map, trying to add to it from memory.

Gabriel Oak

During a lengthy opening description Hardy says that Gabriel Oak's *moral color* is *a kind of pepper-and-salt mixture*; he is a good man but not perfect. Consider this as you read the novel. ✪ Does Gabriel have faults? His clothes tell us that he is a practical man who is outdoors much of the time. His watch has been handed down from father to son, like many of his skills and probably his values as well. He relies as much on the sun and stars as on the watch to tell him the time. ✪ What does this suggest about him?

Gabriel is a good-humored, hard-working countryman, expert in most aspects of farming, and especially sheep. Unlike Troy, he is cautious, and we learn in Chapter 2 that, although he moves quickly when necessary, his movements are usually slow and deliberate. They fit his job and therefore have *elements of grace*. ✪ Think of something you do well that compares to this.

We see him up at night supervizing the lambing, working with Bathsheba to train sheep who have lost their lambs to adopt orphaned lambs, and at the sheepwashing. In one memorable scene, in Chapter 22, we watch him shearing. He flings the frightened ewe over *with a dexterous twist of the arm*, and shears off the complete fleece in record time, without hurting the sheep. In the previous chapter he demonstrates his self-respect by refusing to be at Bathsheba's beck and call after she has dismissed him for giving his honest opinion of her behavior and then shows his expertise in saving her bloated sheep, operating on them *with a dexterity that would have graced a hospital-surgeon.*

THE ANGEL GABRIEL

Gabriel's first name is that of an angel; his surname is that of a tree renowned for its sturdiness and endurance. No wonder, then, that he is the most loyal, reliable, and long-suffering of all the characters in the book. He comes to Bathsheba's aid on other occasions in addition to the incident mentioned above. There is the haystack fire that his knowledge and leadership brings under control (Chapter 6), and the dramatic scene in which he saves her grain from a storm when Troy has gotten the men drunk (Chapter 37). Less obviously, there is his unobtrusive watching over her in her late night rounds of the farm, as well as his tireless labors as her estate manager.

As well as being practically skilled, reliable, and devoted, Gabriel is a man of deep feeling and imagination. Seeing Bathsheba partly obscured by a cloak at night, *his imagination painted her a beauty.* He appreciates the beauty of the night sky, plays the flute, and sings in the choir. Above all, he remains true to his early promise to Bathsheba (Chapter 4): *"I shall do one thing in this life – one thing certain – that is, love you, and long for you, and keep wanting you till I die."* He always loves her, but without the obsessiveness that destroys Boldwood.

NOT QUITE PERFECT

If Gabriel has faults, they are almost virtues compared to Troy's vices. He is rather naïve, at least at first, in taking Bathsheba at her word when she turns him down. He has little idea of how to court a woman, especially one like her. It is also rather foolish of him to admit to spying on her. On the practical side, too, he isn't quite perfect. He nearly suffocates when he lets his hut fill with smoke, his failure to tie up one of his dogs leads to the loss of his flock, and he accidentally cuts a sheep when distracted by his feelings for Bathsheba.

Sergeant Troy

You will find it useful to compare Gabriel with Troy, as Hardy does in Chapter 29:

Troy's deformities lay deep down from a woman's vision, whilst his embellishments were upon the very surface; thus contrasting with homely Oak, whose defects were patent to the blindest, and whose virtues were as metals in a mine.

Whereas you may find it hard to discover any real faults in Gabriel and begin to think he's too good to be true, you might have the opposite problem with Troy. He's not all bad, however. Try defending him. You could make a Mind Map of his good points, and of the factors explaining why he behaves as he does.

THE SEXY SERGEANT

It's obvious why a young country woman would go for him. He's a handsome young soldier, educated, charming, and self-confident. He bristles with masculine energy, and knows how to steal hearts with eloquent and shameless flattery. Unlike solid, cautious Gabriel, planning for the future, building on the past, Troy lives in the present. He is excitingly unpredictable – and very sexy.

He promises to marry Fanny, probably just to seduce her or shut her up, and then claims he has forgotten to arrange it (Chapter 11, at the barracks). His attitude is so careless that this may even be true. When she arrives late at the church (Chapter 16), he regards this as reason enough to abandon her. Compare his attitude toward marriage to that of Gabriel, who first decides that he can afford it, spells out to Bathsheba exactly how it will be, then, on losing his flock, thanks God that he's not married, because he wouldn't want his wife to suffer.

Troy meets Bathsheba at night, by chance, and immediately turns on the charm. This continues at the haymaking, when he cleverly presents himself as Bathsheba's helpless victim, and then when he helps with her bees. He is a bold opportunist, as one might expect a soldier to be. The nearest he gets to planning is arranging to demonstrate his swordplay to Bathsheba, which he does in *The Hollow amid the Ferns*. He is an artist with the sword, just as Gabriel is with the sheep shears, but the sword is a lot more dangerous, and a dangerous man can be very exciting to a young woman.

THE BAD HUSBAND

Once Troy is married, we see him at his worst. He lies to Boldwood merely to taunt him, as a cat might play with a mouse (Chapter 34), and he nearly ruins Bathsheba financially by not getting her grain covered, and then getting the men too drunk to help save it from a storm. She manages her money carefully; he gambles it away. The best that can be said about him is that it's difficult to see how he could find useful employment in a place like Weatherbury—his only skills lie in soldiering and seduction.

To his credit, he does try to help Fanny when he finds out she's pregnant, but at Bathsheba's expense. When Fanny dies, he suddenly becomes devoted to her, treating Bathsheba monstrously in the process.

Troy is not so much an evil man as one who has almost no concept of morality or responsibility. He admits to Bathsheba that he has behaved badly (Chapter 43, *Fanny's Revenge*), but he shows no inclination to make it up to her – only to the dead Fanny. When his first faltering steps toward being a good man, as he sees it, are thwarted by the gargoyle washing away the flowers he has planted on Fanny's grave, he simply gives up: ... *the merest opposition had disheartened him.*

❂ Does it seem cowardly of him to leave Weatherbury as he does and then to go to America, leaving Bathsheba uncertain whether he is dead or alive? When he returns he shows no concern for Bathsheba. He just wants to get his hands on her money and prevent Boldwood from having her. ❂ What is your final judgment of him? Does he deserve his fate?

Farmer Boldwood

A rich, handsome, middle-aged farmer, almost a squire, Boldwood is a very eligible bachelor. In Chapter 12 Hardy writes of him: *He was erect in attitude, and quiet in demeanour. One characteristic pre-eminently marked him – dignity.* Bear this in mind as you read the novel. See how much he changes. Think about his name, too. ❂ Is he bold? Is his manner rather wooden?

We first see Boldwood making concerned inquiries about Fanny Robin, so we know he is either a caring man or one with a sense of social responsibility. Then we find him not noticing Bathsheba at market or in church when everyone else does. We learn from Liddy that he is a solitary type. Rumor has it that he's single because he was once bitterly disappointed in love. Ironically, although this isn't true, it will become so.

NO JOKER

Boldwood is a serious-minded, rather humorless man. He has ... *no light or careless touches to his constitution, either for good or for evil* (Chapter 18). When he receives an anonymous valentine from Bathsheba (Chapter 14), it never occurs to him that it might be a joke, because he would never send one himself – and certainly not as a joke. He easily becomes obsessed, first with the card, and then its sender.

Like Gabriel, Boldwood is naïve when it comes to women. Unlike Troy, he never really woos Bathsheba, and he never tells her that she's beautiful until it's too late. Despite his intense feelings, he makes her a very formal proposal (Chapter 19), with nothing to soften her feelings or arouse her interest.

He also shows a complete lack of insight into her character when he offers her a life of ease and dependence.

DESPAIR

Boldwood is persistent in his attempts to win Bathsheba, but when his hopes are dashed by Troy, he reacts with jealous fury and then despair. Caught in a torment of obsessive love, he throws away his dignity as he offers Troy money first to marry Fanny and then to marry Bathsheba when it seems that she has given herself to him. He wins only Troy's sneering contempt.

Boldwood becomes a man without purpose, neglecting his farm, until Troy's apparent death raises his hopes anew. He becomes fixated on the idea of marrying Bathsheba after the legally required six years. ❂ Does it seem strange that he is prepared to wait so long? His persistence continues, and Bathsheba eventually gives in.

After Boldwood's fatal explosion of passion in Chapter 53, we learn that he has kept a locked closet full of expensive presents for Bathsheba in the hopes of her marrying him. This is evidence – if any were needed – of his sad and self-destructive obsession and of the feelings he has kept locked up inside.

Bathsheba Everdene

The glittering prize that causes so much unintended suffering is the beautiful Bathsheba. We first see her dressed in red (signifying danger, like Troy's uniform, and the seal on the valentine) in her carriage as she approaches Norcombe. Thus, our first view is of an independent woman on the move. Though young, she sticks up for herself in a man's world, as we see when she refuses to pay the toll taker what he asks. This first encounter also reveals Bathsheba's main weakness— she is vain.

Her optimism and opinion of herself help her to reject Gabriel's proposal. She believes she can do better, and besides, she doesn't love him. Her courage and confidence enable her to take charge of the farm she inherits, firing a dishonest manager and taking over his duties herself. She is generally thought to be doing something unnatural in attempting to do a man's job, even if she is grudgingly admired for the way she does it. Even Hardy seems to share this view in part, until Troy starts to drag her down. As you read the novel, decide for yourself what Hardy's attitude is.

WHIMS

Toward the end of the novel, Gabriel calls Bathsheba *skittish*, meaning that she is unpredictable and led by whims that he has had to follow. This is a feature of her character, though less so as she develops. A prime example is when she foolishly sends a valentine, wanting to punish Boldwood for not noticing her. This act sets off a fatal chain of events.

Another example of her impulsiveness is firing Gabriel for giving her his opinion of her behavior. Here is another feature of her character: pride. She hates being told she's wrong, especially by an employee, and even more so because she knows he's right. However, she has enough humility to request his help politely when he refuses to be ordered (Chapter 21), even adding the words *"Do not desert me, Gabriel,"* and asking him to stay on after all.

SLAVE TO LOVE

It is humiliating to such a proud and independent woman to become a slave to love, as she does when seduced by Troy. She marries him out of fear that he will leave her for another woman, and she regrets it almost at once, although she loves him so much that when he kisses Fanny in her coffin, she frantically begs him to kiss her as well.

For all her pride, vanity, and impulsiveness, Bathsheba has some fine qualities. She deeply regrets the pain she has caused Boldwood, and even considers marrying him to make up for it. She is loyal to Troy and generous enough first to tend the grave of his dead lover and then to have him buried next to her (Chapters 46 and 56).

Victorian women

Bathsheba's independent role is seen as very unusual. Hardy may occasionally seem sexist, but he was enlightened for his time. He shows Bathsheba coping well in her role, and he arouses our sympathy for the plight of women like her who have bad husbands, and like Fanny who are seduced with promises and then abandoned. Even so, Hardy conforms to Victorian expectations. The happy ending comes only when Bathsheba realizes that she needs a man to lean on and that she could never have survived without Gabriel.

Fanny Robin

Fanny is Bathsheba's youngest servant. In Chapter 7 she encounters Gabriel. He doesn't know it, but she is planning to go off with Troy. Her voice is *the low and dulcet note suggestive of romance*, but her pulse beats with *a tragic intensity*, and she is a *slight and fragile creature*. The way Hardy describes her in Chapter 11, as she approaches Casterbridge barracks, emphasizes her smallness. She is a pathetic figure, gullible and unable to assert or support herself.

She shows courage and determination in her last journey as she drags herself along the Casterbridge highway to the workhouse (Chapter 40), but even then she only makes it by tricking herself and with the help of a large dog. She only has any real power when she is in her coffin.

Liddy

Liddy plays a role in the plot as a supplier of information—the gossip she provides about Boldwood and Troy and the rumor about Fanny's baby. She also represents the more silly, girlish, irresponsible side of Bathsheba and encourages her to send the valentine. However, she does carry some weight as a real character. She copies Bathsheba's stately exit in a slightly mocking way (Chapter 10), stands up for herself and threatens to leave when Bathsheba treats her unfairly (Chapter 30), and gives Bathsheba emotional support after Troy leaves. She is also a sympathetic confidante when Bathsheba decides to marry Gabriel.

The rustics

The ordinary country working people – or "rustics" – act as a kind of chorus (as found in ancient Greek tragedy, and some Shakespearean plays, such as *Macbeth*), supplying information and commenting on the major characters. They also provide light entertainment.

In Chapter 8, Hardy introduces them all in turn. For example, there is Henery, who insists on spelling his name as he pronounces it, the timid Joseph Poorgrass, who once had a terrified conversation with an owl, and the henpecked *Susan Tall's husband*.

The rustics aren't always tactful. Henery tells Gabriel that when he plays the flute his mouth is *scrimped up* and his eyes stare *like a strangled man's*. There is comic **irony** in Hardy's description of Joseph's *winning suavity* in reassuring Gabriel that he is a handsome man. (The irony is in Hardy making a joke at Joseph's expense by pretending to think him suave, or sophisticated.)

Trembling Joseph Poorgrass and henpecked Laban Tall play occasional roles elsewhere. In Chapter 42, Joseph's failure to deliver Fanny's coffin leads to the tempestuous scene involving Troy, Bathsheba, and the dead Fanny. Jan Coggan is also relatively important, as Gabriel's second-in-command and confidante. He organizes the makeshift wedding reception that makes the novel's happy ending complete.

How's it going so far?

? Draw your own icons for the main characters, perhaps using items you associate with them or that are associated with their names. (Or draw the characters themselves.) Put them on a sheet of paper. Around each, write key words to describe them, scenes that show their traits particularly well, and anything you think they might say about themselves.

? Test yourself using the Mini Mind Map on p. 6 and the full Mind Map on p. 15, as suggested at the beginning of the chapter.

now that you know who's who, take a break before finding out what's what

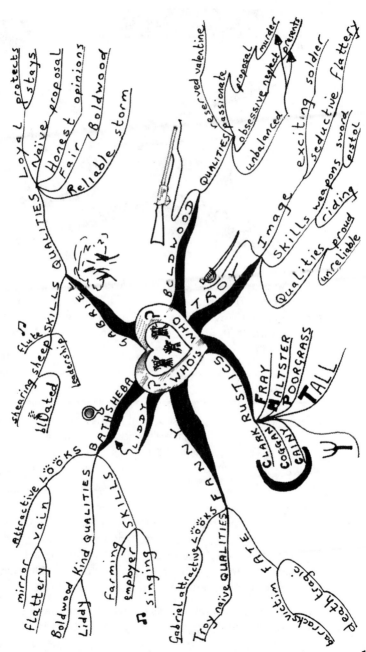

THEMES

A theme is an idea developed or explored throughout a work. The Mini Mind Map above shows the main themes of *Far from the Madding Crowd*. Test yourself by copying the Mini Mind Map, adding to it, and then comparing your results with the version on p. 24.

Love

In describing Boldwood's situation, Hardy comments that he has no sister, mother, or casual girlfriends on whom his affections can focus. This suggests that there might be different elements of feeling in romantic love. ✪ Think for a moment about what these are.

Romantic love – whether deep and lasting, obsessive, or sexually passionate – is the main driving force in *Far from the Madding Crowd*. It is the single most important reason for the characters behaving as they do. The main focus is Bathsheba, who is actually compared to Aphrodite, goddess of love. Of course, she is also one of the lovers, and Fanny also plays a role.

Hardy explores several aspects of love. As with the theme of Men and Women (see p. 18), he does this both in direct comments and through what the characters do and say. He also does it indirectly in imagery, especially of nature (see separate entry, p. 20), and in the recurring use of the color red, which stands for passion and the danger that goes with it.

Note, memorize (ideas if not actual words), and consider the following quotes:

> ... there is no regular path for getting out of love as there is for getting in. Some people look upon marriage as a shortcut that way, but it has been known to fail. (Chapter 5)

> This good-fellowship ... proves itself to be the only love which is strong as death – that love which many waters cannot quench, nor the floods drown, beside which the passion usually called by the name is evanescent as steam. (Chapter 56, last paragraph)

The first quote is a slightly cynical comment on how one can be trapped by love and on how marriage can put an end to it. This is echoed in Troy's line in Chapter 41, *"All romances end in marriage."* ✪ Why might there be some truth in this? (Note that sex before marriage was relatively rare when this book was written.) The second quote is a comment on the kind of love, based on long friendship and shared work, achieved by Gabriel and Bathsheba. Hardy compares it here with being "in love."

The first hint of love comes when Gabriel begins to fall for Bathsheba. His proposal is described humorously. His attempts to make himself presentable are rather silly and so is the conversation he and Bathsheba hold through the holly bush (see Chapter 4, and Commentary, p. 29).

Bathsheba toys with the idea of love when she sends Boldwood the all-important valentine with its blood-red seal. We see another side of love when he becomes obsessed with her, crazy in love, and she cries, *"How was I to know that what is a pastime to all other men was death to you?"* Boldwood does seem to care about her, but above all, he feels he cannot live without her. His need is real, but rather selfish.

To Troy, love certainly is *a pastime*, a matter of sexual conquest, though he also does have a streak of romanticism that emerges when Fanny dies. Gabriel, on the other hand, never treats love lightly. Love makes him noble. For love, he sticks by Bathsheba throughout all her problems, but he remains his own man, never giving in to despair the way Boldwood does.

Loyalty

The theme of love is closely linked to that of loyalty. Gabriel is always loyal to Bathsheba, though he never loses his self-respect as a result. He criticizes her when he thinks it's justified, and at the end of the book he even considers emigrating. Hardy comments: *Women are never tired of bewailing man's fickleness in love, but they only seem to snub his constancy.* Boldwood is loyal to Bathsheba, but obsessively so. Troy never shows her the slightest hint of loyalty. He belatedly makes an effort to help Fanny when she's pregnant, but in the end, even Fanny owes more to the dog that helps her reach the workhouse than to Troy.

Some nonromantic examples of loyalty are worth remembering: Coggan's to Gabriel, Liddy's to Bathsheba, and the mutual loyalty and sense of duty between Bathsheba and her workers.

Men and women

You may not be asked on an exam for your own views on the differences in the relationships between men and women or on sexism. However, it's worth thinking about them so that you can see Hardy's treatment of this important theme more clearly.

The book is peppered with Hardy's comments on the differences between the sexes, on women, and on how the behavior of particular characters typifies their sex. Most are given directly from author to reader, but some are put into the mouths of characters. The character most commonly held up as typical is Bathsheba. Hardy talks about men less, seeming to take male behavior as the standard from which women deviate. So, for example, he mentions in Chapter 31 ... *woman's privileges in tergiversation,* meaning that women change their minds a lot. He doesn't consider it normal to change one's mind, and comments on men's obstinate refusal to do so!

Here are a few of Hardy's comments. Note, memorize (ideas if not actual words), and consider:

> *It appears that ordinary men take wives because possession is not possible without marriage, and that ordinary women accept husbands because marriage is not possible without possession.* (Chapter 20 – By *possession* he means sex, as well as ownership in a more general sense.)

> *Bathsheba, though she had too much understanding to be entirely governed by her womanliness, had too much womanliness to use her understanding to the best advantage.* (Chapter 29, paragraph 1)

> *"It is difficult for a woman to define her feelings in language which is chiefly made by men to express theirs."* (Bathsheba to Boldwood, Chapter 51)

The other way in which the theme emerges is in how the male and female characters behave. Much of this you may recall from the Who's Who? section of this guide. Look especially at how far they play out conventional male and female roles, or conform to stereotypes.

Bathsheba is vain, contradictory, impulsive, and given to changing her mind. She puzzles the rustics by being so good at doing the "man's job" of running a farm and its business. She's brave and independent, but loses much of her self-reliance and self-respect when she falls into Troy's clutches.

Liddy and **Fanny** are much less important women. Liddy is a stereotypical female type: the gossip. Fanny is weak, passive, and a victim, another very negative female stereotype.

Gabriel and **Boldwood** conform to much of what is conventionally expected of a man. Both are protectors of women, Gabriel more effectively than Boldwood. Neither has much understanding of women at first, but Gabriel learns a great deal during the course of the novel.

Troy plays another familiar male role, one common in Victorian melodrama. He is the smooth-talking seducer and exploiter of women. He understands them only as an expert hunter understands his prey. To Troy, women are sport. Despite being what is commonly called a "lady's man," he is actually more at home in the world of men – the army barracks, the racetrack, or the harvest supper after he has sent the women home to bed.

Nature

❂ Do you enjoy Hardy's descriptions of nature, or just skip over them? Try to think of one example. On one level, they are like the scenery on a country walk. There is the wonderful picture that he creates in Chapter 2 of night on Norcombe Hill (see Commentary, p. 27), or his account of the first day of June, when *Every green was young, every pore was open, and every stalk was swollen with racing currents of juice* (Chapter 22, paragraph 2). He reels off a list of plants that shows his knowledge as a country man. However, all this would be little more than wallpaper to the plot were it not for the way in which Hardy uses it.

At this point you must grasp the meaning of two important terms: **setting** and **atmosphere**. "Setting" means the place in which the action occurs, for example, the malthouse or the woods, together with anything affecting that place at the time, particularly the weather. "Atmosphere" is the mood that a writer creates, both by action and dialogue and by use of the setting. Hardy often uses natural settings to create atmosphere and underline what is happening in the story.

One important way in which he does this is in the timing of events according to the seasons. (See the plot flowchart, p. 5.) Gabriel meets and eventually marries Bathsheba in midwinter. Troy, on the other hand, meets her in early summer, marries her in midsummer, and has abandoned her by the fall of the same year. Theirs is a fair-weather romance, not built to withstand difficult times. It lasts while nature is in full bloom, reflecting the heat of their sexual attraction, and withers with the leaves on the trees. Compare *the hollow amid the ferns* in summer (Chapter 28) with what is probably the same place, in the fall, after Troy has left (Chapter 44; Commentary, p. 64). Notice, too, how the nearby swamp reflects the danger and corruption in her relationship with Troy.

Natural events also show the characters in their true light. An important example of this is Gabriel's prediction of the storm (Nature is here personified as sending him messages), and his pitting himself against it to protect the grain. See Chapters 36 and 37 (Commentary, pp. 55–57). Gabriel understands nature; Troy's interest is limited to the rain spoiling his chances at the races. The storm also reflects what is going on in the emotions of the main characters.

Time and change

In *Far from the Madding Crowd*, time is seen in three main ways. First, it is the **agent of change**. In this sense it ties in with the seasons (see Nature, above). Scenes change from day to night (Chapters 1 and 2), and season to season; people change as a result of their experiences, and relationships begin, flower, and either wither or bear fruit. Sometimes these changes are shown in the imagery of nature. See the description of the moon still visible at sunrise, reflecting the unhealthy changes in Boldwood (Chapter 14), or the differences between the scenery in Chapters 28 (*The Hollow amid the Ferns*) and 44 (*Under a Tree – Reaction*).

Second, time is the ever-changing **moment**. Gabriel has a well-developed sense of time. He appreciates the beauty of the night sky, but it also serves him as a clock. Read the paragraph in Chapter 2 beginning, *The Dog-star and Aldebaran*, followed by Gabriel's confident *"One o'clock."* Much is made of Gabriel's watch, handed down from father to son. We might compare this with Troy's somewhat more elegant watch, which he gives to Bathsheba and then takes back again; a man who first gives and then takes back his time cannot be relied on.

In fact, Troy couldn't do without his watch. He's rather particular about punctuality. He makes Fanny come to his barracks at ten o'clock. Then he deserts her when she's half an hour late for their wedding. Chapter 16, *All Saints' and All Souls*, focuses on this second episode, and especially on the little model man linked to the clock, striking a bell each quarter hour. This *quarter-jack* becomes a symbol of time itself, mocking mankind with its *malicious leer*.

Third, we see time as **age**. In this role it usually commands respect, as with the old maltster (brewer) who figures his age to be 117 (Chapter 8), or the shearing-barn (Chapter 22), which *embodied practices which had suffered no mutilation at the hands of time.*

The Church and blind chance

In an age in which science was advancing in England, and the Church was declining, Hardy became uncertain in his beliefs about religion and the Church. He was deeply conscious of the role blind chance played in the lives of human beings, and beginning with this book, Hardy explored in six major novels his favorite theme: the terrible price human beings pay for seemingly trivial actions. The tragic consequences in this story might never have happened if Gabriel had shut his dog indoors, if Fanny had gone to the right church for her wedding, if Troy's spurs had not caught in Bathsheba's dress, or if Bathsheba had sent her playful valentine to someone other than the volcanic Boldwood. Hardy believed that these actions in themselves were unimportant, that a merciful God would have forgiven them as petty follies. Caught up in the process of blind chance, however, small mistakes become launching pads leading to terrible and undeserved punishments.

Churches are rarely mentioned in this novel. On the first page, Gabriel, who is by far the most upstanding person in the book, is said to occupy the middle space between the Communion people of the parish and the *drunken section* at the malthouse. He regularly goes to church, but he yawns privately and wonders what there will be for dinner instead of listening to the sermon. The rustic farm laborers, all *staunch Church of England*, talk humorously about the Church over their drinks at the pub, one saying, *"I've stuck like a plaster to the old faith I was born in."* He adds that a man can belong to the Church and stay in his cheerful old malthouse *"and never trouble or worry his mind about doctrines at all."* Also, Fanny goes to the wrong church for her wedding, and Gabriel and Bathsheba, in the last chapter, walk to the little church to be wed, but formal religion receives far less mention than the awful workings of fate and chance.

Craft

There are many occasions when Hardy makes us admire human ability to become expertly skilled. For example, his knowledgeable descriptions of architecture show how he appreciates the skills of the architect and the stonemason. More important, though, are the demonstrations given by his characters.

Gabriel is remarkably capable. See his saving of Bathsheba's bloated sheep (Chapter 21), his sheep shearing (Chapter 22), and the scenes in which he saves her fields from fire and rain (Chapters 6 and 37). More surprisingly, he and Coggan also turn out to be expert trackers (Chapter 32). Whereas Gabriel wields the shears, **Troy** shows his special skill in swordsmanship, though he is also an excellent rider and marksman. **Bathsheba** excels at farm management and business, as well as practical farming tasks.

Progress check

? Draw all the theme icons across a sheet of paper. Think about how the themes are connected. For example, loyalty and time are linked, because loyalty is remaining true to someone over a long period of time. Draw connecting lines and label them with key words to show the connections.

? Think of three examples of "setting" in *Far from the Madding Crowd*. Draw an image to represent each. Around your image, write key words to suggest the atmosphere created by that setting.

? Test yourself by using the Mini Mind Map and full Mind Map, as suggested at the beginning of this chapter.

now you know what's what; take a break before the blow-by-blow account

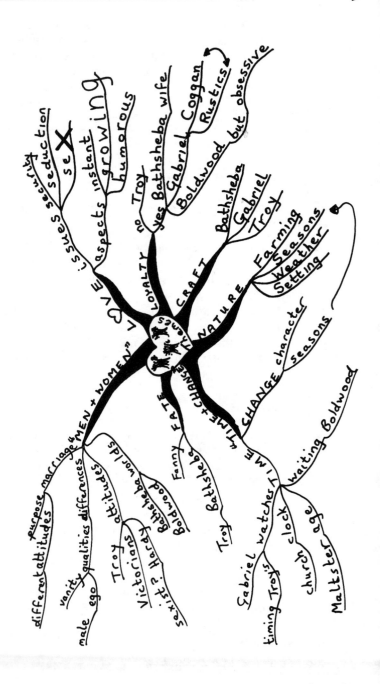

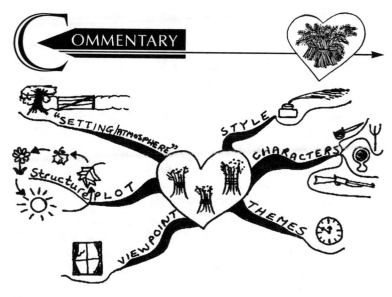

COMMENTARY

The Commentary looks at each chapter in turn, beginning with a brief preview that will prepare you for the chapter and help with review. The Commentary discusses whatever is important in the chapter, focusing on the areas shown in the Mini Mind Map above.

ICONS

Wherever there is a focus on a particular theme, the icon for that theme appears in the margin (see p. ix for key). Look out, too, for the Style and Language sections. Being able to comment on style and language will help you to get an "A" on your exam.

You will learn more from the Commentary if you use it alongside the novel itself. Read a chapter from the novel, then the corresponding Commentary section – or the other way around.

QUESTIONS

Remember that whenever a question appears in the Commentary with a star ✪ in front of it, you should stop and think about it for a moment. And **do remember to take a break** after completing each exercise.

Chapter 1 *Description of Farmer Oak – An Incident*

◆ Description of Gabriel's appearance.
◆ Gabriel sees Bathsheba in her wagon and watches her look at herself in the mirror.
◆ Gabriel pays the toll taker when Bathsheba refuses to.

Our first impression of Gabriel Oak is of a good-natured and happy man. Much of the chapter focuses on his appearance, which Hardy uses to suggest his character. The wrinkles around his eyes are like the rays of the rising sun. ✸ Why is this image appropriate for a good-natured farmer?

Rounding off the description with the information that Gabriel is 28 and a bachelor, Hardy describes a scene: Gabriel is on Norcombe Hill when he sees a yellow wagon approaching. It contains Bathsheba and everything she owns. ✸ What does this first appearance suggest about her?

✐ STYLE AND LANGUAGE

Notice how Hardy draws us into the scene. We see Bathsheba through Gabriel's eyes, though the words are Hardy's. We hear the wagon driver's steps grow faint and see the wagon's contents as Hardy describes them in detail, including the cat and the canary.

Reread the paragraphs where Bathsheba looks at herself in a mirror. Hardy says that *Woman's prescriptive infirmity had stalked into the sunlight*. Notice the **metaphor**, centering on the rather unusual choice of the word *stalked*. It's a metaphor because woman's *infirmity* is spoken of as if it is a creature, not something abstract. The "infirmity" is vanity. ✸ Gabriel thinks she's vain. Do you? Do you think Hardy sees vanity as a female trait? Bear this question in mind as you read on.

Gabriel pays the toll for using the road when Bathsheba thinks it's too much. She barely looks at him. ✸ What does the incident tell you about them both?

Chapter 2 *Night–The Flock–An Interior–Another Interior*

◆ Description of Norcombe Hill on a windy night.
◆ Gabriel plays the flute in his hut and tends his sheep.
◆ Description of Gabriel's becoming a farmer.
◆ Description of the hut.
◆ Gabriel sees a light and watches Bathsheba in the cowshed.

The chapter alternates between description and action. Hardy builds up atmosphere by describing a scene so that we almost feel as if we're there.

Time is stressed in this chapter, which begins with *It was nearly midnight* (the middle of the night for country people then). It is midwinter. Norcombe Hill is now cold, dark, and desolate. Hardy likes to show how things change, and this change brought on by nature is a good example.

STYLE AND LANGUAGE

Hardy describes the wind blowing through the *ancient and decaying plantation of beeches*. The wind flounders, grumbles, and gushes *in a weakened moan*; the leaves simmer and boil in the breezes. The whole scene is alive and constantly changing. The description of the trees chanting to each other like a cathedral choir makes it seem almost like a place of worship.

Hardy describes the stars and the sense of wonder they can bring. Then he brings us back to the story with *an unexpected series of sounds*. It is Gabriel's flute. ✪ What effect is achieved by reintroducing Gabriel this way, with the sound first, then its explanation? Look for this technique; Hardy often uses it.

We then see inside Gabriel's lambing hut and hear how he has become a farmer, an occupation to which he is well suited. We see Gabriel tending a lamb inside his practical but cozy hut. He seems to be gentle as well as skilled. His observation of the stars shows his knowledge and use of nature, but he also sees the starry sky *as a work of art superlatively beautiful*.

Gabriel sees a light that comes from a cowshed where Bathsheba is tending a cow and calf. This is the second time that Gabriel has spied on Bathsheba. He sees her *in a bird's-eye view, as Milton's Satan first saw Paradise*. This refers to Milton's *Paradise Lost*. We discover later that this is one of Gabriel's few books. Satan was an angel cast out from heaven. ✪ How appropriate is the image here?

Chapter 3 *A Girl on Horseback – Conversation*

◆ Bathsheba looks for her hat.
◆ Gabriel watches her riding.
◆ Gabriel finds the hat, gives it back, and tells Bathsheba he's seen her.
◆ Bathsheba saves Gabriel from suffocation. She refuses to reveal her name.

Gabriel is once again in the beech plantation when he sees Bathsheba on horseback. He guesses that she is probably looking for her hat, finds it himself, and returns to his hut.

Gabriel is surprised and amused to see Bathsheba riding like a circus performer. When he sees her again she has *a bright air and manner* about her, as if she feels pleased with herself. Hardy describes her at length, even long-windedly, saying that some Englishwomen have a beautiful face, some a good figure, but that Bathsheba is one of the few with both. ✪ What do you think of this comment?

Bathsheba is modest as well as beautiful. Like any polite country girl, she wouldn't be seen in a low-cut dress, and when Gabriel looks at her, she self-consciously brushes at her face. She blushes deeply when he tells her that he's been watching her. He turns away to spare her further embarrassment, and she quietly leaves, offended.

The scene in which Gabriel nearly suffocates shows that he can make mistakes and that Bathsheba is capable of quick, sensible action. He regains consciousness with his head in her lap. This romantic scene helps to establish a relationship.

Bathsheba refuses to reveal her name to Gabriel. ❂ Is she just being haughty because she thinks she's better than Gabriel, or is she flirting with him? She teases him and says he can kiss her hand, then snatches it back before he does. ❂ What are your impressions of Gabriel and Bathsheba so far?

Chapter 4 *Gabriel's Resolve–The Visit–The Mistake*

◆ Gabriel goes to court Bathsheba.
◆ She says she cannot marry him.
◆ He declares his undying love.

Gabriel Oak is falling in love with Bathsheba. He discovers her name and resolves to make her his wife. When he goes to visit her he dresses up and puts so much oil on his hair that its color is a cross between birds' droppings and cement. It sticks to his head like seaweed. ❂ What impression is this likely to make?

The visit gets off to a bad start when Gabriel's dog frightens Bathsheba's cat. Gabriel speaks to Mrs. Hurst, Bathsheba's aunt, and almost immediately says that he wants to marry Bathsheba. When she says her niece has lots of young men interested in her, Gabriel gives up at once. ❂ Is he being realistic, modest, defeatist, or stupid?

The scene that follows, in which Gabriel proposes, marks another stage in their relationship. Bathsheba runs after him in a very unladylike manner, becoming as pink as a peony petal. Gabriel assumes that she wants to marry him. There is humor in the way Bathsheba's hand slips through Gabriel's fingers *like an eel* and in their conversation held through a holly bush. Picture the scene in order to remember it.

Gabriel's way of courting is to tell Bathsheba exactly what she'll have as his wife. Compare this with Troy's method later and decide which is likely to be more exciting to a young woman like Bathsheba. Ironically, the picture of loyalty and constancy that Gabriel paints is what finally decides Bathsheba against him. ❂ What does Gabriel do wrong?

Chapter 5 *Departure of Bathsheba–A Pastoral Tragedy*

◆ Gabriel hears that Bathsheba has moved to Weatherbury.
◆ Description of Gabriel's dogs.
◆ Gabriel loses his flock.

Hardy often begins a chapter with a general comment on human nature. Here he observes that the more strongly someone says they are giving something up, the less likely they are to stick to their resolve. He applies this to Gabriel, who decides to give up Bathsheba when he hears she has moved away.

Hardy describes Gabriel's two dogs with affection and humor. George, the elder, is an expert sheepdog. When the over-enthusiastic younger dog chases the sheep off a cliff into a chalk pit to their deaths, Gabriel is financially ruined.
✪ Do you think this is just bad luck, or is he to blame for not getting the dog in for the night?

✪ How would you feel in Gabriel's situation? Are you surprised by his first response – *one of pity for these gentle ewes and their unborn lambs?* After this he thinks of the financial loss and how all his work has come to nothing. Even then, he is grateful that he is not married because of the hardship his wife would now have to suffer.

✐ STYLE AND LANGUAGE

Notice the use of imagery after the sheep have died. The moon is like an *attenuated skeleton* "dogged" by the morning star. The pool glitters *like a dead man's eye.*

Test yourself

? Circle any words or phrases below that describe Gabriel. Use another color for those that describe Bathsheba. Underline any that describe both.

haughty   naïve   vain   optimistic
hard-working   country-born   skillful
conscientious   unconventional   observant
musical   easily embarrassed   kind to animals

? ? How does each thing above feature in the story so far? Mind Map the advice you would give to a young man intending to court Bathsheba.

Time for you to do what poor Gabriel can't afford to do now – Take a break!

Chapter 6 *The Fair – The Journey – The Fire*

◆ Gabriel fails to get work at the hiring fair.
◆ He sets off for another fair, riding some of the way in a wagon.
◆ He takes charge of fighting a haystack fire.
◆ He asks the owner – Bathsheba – for work.

THE HIRING FAIR

The chapter begins at the hiring fair, with the laborers *waiting upon Chance*. Chance – or Fate – has dealt Gabriel a cruel blow in the loss of his sheep. He has sunk *from ... pastoral king into the very slime-pits of Siddim* (into which some biblical kings fell). Now he can't even get work. The farmers shun him like the plague, thinking him *too good to be trustworthy*. ○ Why do you suppose this is?

Gabriel earns a few pence playing his flute, and hears of another hiring fair at Weatherbury. By another twist of fate, this is where Bathsheba has gone. He sets off and falls asleep in a hay wagon on the way. Fate is at work again; the wagon is Bathsheba's, and Gabriel awakes to find its drivers discussing their mistress.

THE HAY FIRE

 Gabriel comes across a haystack fire that threatens to spread. The disorganized farm workers have little hope of putting out the fire. Gabriel shows intelligence, courage, and leadership in taking charge. He also shows a mastery of nature; he knows that he must cut off the fire's air supply.

Bathsheba is astonished to find that the man who has saved her hay is the one who recently proposed to her. The final line, *"Do you want a shepherd, m'am?"* is pathetic in that Gabriel has to ask her for work, but it is also ironic: she needs someone to guide her, not just her sheep.

✒ STYLE AND LANGUAGE

This night scene is very visual. Hardy describes the burning hay like *knots of red worms*, the sparks flying *in clusters like birds from a nest*, and the dancing shadows of the fire fighters. Try to picture the scene, and the images used to describe it.

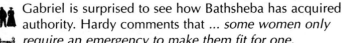

Chapter 7 *Recognition – A Timid Girl*

◆ Bathsheba agrees to hire Gabriel.
◆ Gabriel meets Fanny Robin.

Bathsheba is persuaded to hire Gabriel as a shepherd. As before, Bathsheba is described – with a little irony – as a goddess, this time the familiar goddess of love, Venus. (Ashtoreth was another version of the same goddess.)

Gabriel is surprised to see how Bathsheba has acquired authority. Hardy comments that ... *some women only require an emergency to make them fit for one.*

We get a hint of the farm manager Pennyways' character when he refuses to help Gabriel find a lodging for the night.

Gabriel meets a slim, thinly clothed girl with an attractive voice and gives her a shilling. We get an indication of things to come when we hear that her pulse beats *with a throb of tragic intensity* and that Gabriel feels himself to be *in the penumbra of a very deep sadness* when touching her (penumbra means shadow). She is Fanny Robin, who indeed is to become a tragic figure.

> ## Chapter 8 *The Malthouse – The Chat – News*

◆ Gabriel visits the malthouse and meets the locals.
◆ News comes that Bathsheba has fired Pennyways for theft, and that Fanny Robin has disappeared.

This chapter is mostly description and dialogue. Even its two main events, the dismissal of Pennyways and the disappearance of Bathsheba's youngest servant, Fanny, are reported second-hand. However, there is much humor and entertainment in Hardy's affectionate characterization of the "rustics" – the local working people. Although idealized, it is based on Hardy's own experience of country life.

The malthouse is a place where barley malt is made. The barley has to be warm, so the malthouse is cozy and becomes a sort of village social club. Gabriel is accepted here and given respect as the man who saved the hay and as a skilled shepherd. He gains even more acceptance when the old maltster realizes that he knew Gabriel's family; Gabriel comes from a long line of local shepherds. ✪ Why does this make a difference? Is he lucky to be accepted so quickly? What do you think of the men's standards of hygiene?

GABRIEL'S BOOKS

At the end of the chapter, Gabriel is thinking fondly of Bathsheba (who has stopped in briefly) and planning to get his few possessions, including his books. ✪ How does the list of books reflect his character and lifestyle?

Chapter 9 *The Homestead–A Visitor–Half-Confidences*

◆ Bathsheba's new home is described.
◆ We meet the female members of Bathsheba's household.
◆ Boldwood calls to ask about Fanny, but Bathsheba cannot receive him.

In the detailed description of Bathsheba's big old country house, we see Hardy's detailed knowledge of architecture. ❂ Do you think he gives too much detail?

Within the house, we see a complete contrast to the male world of the last chapter. But while Bathsheba was allowed to intrude in the malthouse, the male visitor to her female world – the gentleman farmer Boldwood – is sent away, because the vain Bathsheba doesn't want him to see her not looking well.

We meet Bathsheba's maid-companion Liddy, a lively young woman equal to Bathsheba in age but not in depth of character, and the servants Maryann and Mrs. Coggan. Liddy tells Bathsheba that Boldwood is handsome, rich, and a confirmed bachelor. This rouses Bathsheba's interest, and she is irritated at not being able to meet him. ❂ Why is she interested in a man who seems determined to stay single?

Chapter 10 *Mistress and Men*

◆ Bathsheba tells her workers that she has dismissed Pennyways and will run the farm herself. She asks about Fanny.
◆ She asks all the workers what they do and pays them.
◆ News comes that Fanny has gone off with a soldier.
◆ Bathsheba declares her intention to astonish them all.

In this scene, Bathsheba shows the traditionally male qualities of authority and determination, coupled with concern for Fanny, interest in her workers, and fairness – even generosity (Joseph's bonus). She doesn't allow Henery Fray to worm his way into her favor, and she shocks Gabriel with her formality. ❂ Has she become "stuck up," or just businesslike? Why does Liddy imitate her exit?

"RUN AWAY WITH THE SOLDIERS"

 Billy Smallbury brings news that will become vital to the plot: Fanny has run off with her soldier-lover's regiment.

● Why might a country town be stirred by a regiment's departure? What's attractive about soldiers? Although we don't know it yet, this is the first mention of a character who will become very important – Sergeant Troy.

Flex your memory muscles

? Who has sunk *into the very slime-pits of Siddim* (Chapter 6)?

What does Hardy compare to *knots of red worms* (Chapter 6)?

Whose pulse beats *with a throb of tragic intensity* (Chapter 7)?

Who has risen *from a cottage to a large house and fields* (Chapter 10)?

? Write one or more sentences that might be spoken about Bathsheba by (1) Liddy, (2) Joseph Poorgrass, (3) Pennyways. The pictures should help.

now that you've seen Bathsheba take charge, take a break before seeing more of a very different kind of woman

Chapter 11 *Outside the Barracks – Snow – A Meeting*

◆ Description of the barracks on a snowy night.
◆ Fanny attracts Troy's attention. They discuss marriage.

Much of this chapter consists of atmospheric description, as in Chapter 2. The scene is dark and dreary, cold and snowy. This adds to the pathos of the lonely, frail, and trusting Fanny Robin talking to Troy across the river by which they are divided, as they will eventually be by death. It is hard to imagine anything good coming out of this depressing scene. It **foreshadows** (warns us of) things to come.

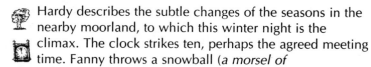 Hardy describes the subtle changes of the seasons in the nearby moorland, to which this winter night is the climax. The clock strikes ten, perhaps the agreed meeting time. Fanny throws a snowball (*a morsel of snow* matching her size and strength) to get Troy's attention. ✪ Hardy comments that *No man ... could possibly have thrown with such utter imbecility.* Is he being sexist?

Troy does not seem pleased to see Fanny, or even sympathetic. He seems reluctant to marry her, and says he has forgotten to arrange it. ✪ How do you feel about Fanny's apology: *"It was wrong of me to worry you ...?"* How do you feel about Troy so far? And why is there laughter from within the barracks?

✒ STYLE AND LANGUAGE

Hardy uses some favorite features here. He builds the scene up impressionistically rather than simply saying what's going on. The second paragraph (*It was a night when sorrow ...*) gives a powerful impression of mood through examples. Also typical is: *If anything could be darker than the sky, it was the wall, and if anything could be gloomier than the wall it was the river beneath.* Each image is replaced in turn by a more intense one. The clock's striking is described as a *succession of dull blows.* Fanny is seen only as a *little shape.* ✪ What effect does this have?

Chapter 12 *Farmers – A Rule – An Exception*

◆ Bathsheba goes to the Casterbridge grain market for the first time.
◆ She observes that one man fails to notice her: Boldwood.

Bathsheba goes to the grain market to trade. This is a man's world. She finds it more difficult than she expects, but she is determined to be taken seriously. Hardy focuses on her femininity and sex appeal, but makes her practical business sense clear. He thinks she succeeds *despite* being a woman: *Strange to say of a woman in full bloom and vigour, she always allowed her interlocutors to finish their statements before rejoining with hers.* On the other hand, she gets other farmers to drop their prices *as was inevitable in a woman.*
❏ What do you think of Hardy's view of women?

The farmers think she's headstrong, but find her attractive – all but one. This *black sheep among the flock* is Boldwood. She is annoyed that he fails to notice her and discreetly finds out from Liddy who he is. ❏ Which rumor about him do you believe at this stage?

Chapter 13 *Sortes Sanctorum – The Valentine*

◆ Bathsheba and Liddy play an old game to find out who Bathsheba will marry.
◆ They discuss Boldwood.
◆ Bathsheba wonders to whom she should send a valentine.
◆ She tosses a hymnal to decide, and sends the card to Boldwood.

One boring Sunday afternoon, Liddy and Bathsheba decide to play a fortune-telling game to see who Bathsheba will marry. Liddy intuitively guesses that Bathsheba was thinking of Boldwood. She tells Bathsheba that Boldwood was ignoring her in church, as if this proves his romantic interest, but Bathsheba doesn't agree, and is still annoyed that Boldwood (like David in the Bible) refuses to worship her. ❏ What do you think of her attitude? Do you know anyone like her?

Still more bored than interested, Bathsheba, for no clear reason, puts herself in the hands of fate and tosses a hymnal to decide who will receive her valentine. ✪ Do you believe that fate somehow decides for her? Even the seal used is accidental (or fated); it says "Marry me."

🖤 Read the final paragraph. ✪ What does Bathsheba's inexperience seem to foretell? From this seemingly harmless joke, tragedy unfolds. Liddy's earlier comment on Boldwood, *He'd worry to death*, is ironic. ✪ Does Bathsheba deserve to suffer for her joke? Why does she play it?

Chapter 14 *Effect of the Letter – Sunrise*

◆ Boldwood sits and contemplates the valentine before going to bed.

◆ He receives a letter for Gabriel, delivered by mistake, and goes to give it to him.

👫 In contrast to Chapter 13's outwardly playful scene in the lively female world of Bathsheba's home, we see the heavy, serious, solitary world of Boldwood. It is the evening of St. Valentine's Day, and Boldwood has received the valentine. He studies it obsessively, wondering who could have sent it.

🖤 ✪ Have you ever sent or received an anonymous valentine? Do you think Boldwood has received one before? Compare his mood with the mood in which it was sent. He feels *uneasy and dissatisfied with himself for his nervous excitability,* as he goes to bed. Why do you suppose it affects him like this, and so deeply?

When he receives a letter that was delivered by mistake, he is already so caught up in the valentine mystery that he expects it to be from the same woman.

✒️ **STYLE AND LANGUAGE**

Boldwood's confusion is reflected in the sunrise that resembles a sunset, and in the *preternatural inversion of light and shade* caused by the snow. Even the waning moon, still in the sky at dawn, seems sinister: *dull and greenish-yellow, like tarnished brass.*

The red wax seal is ominously compared to a *blot of blood* on Boldwood's eye, Gabriel's distant figure to *the black snuff in the midst of a candle-flame.* And there is the sinister feel of the *square skeleton masses* Gabriel carries. These images foreshadow things to come.

Chapter 15 *A Morning Meeting–The Letter Again*

◆ The farm workers discuss Bathsheba in the malthouse.
◆ Gabriel warns them against criticizing her.
◆ Boldwood gives Gabriel the letter, which is from Fanny.
◆ Gabriel discloses its contents to Boldwood.
◆ Gabriel identifies Boldwood's valentine as coming from Bathsheba.

After the seriousness of the last chapter, there is light relief. The toothless old maltster is eating breakfast and is joined by several men. They discuss how Bathsheba is getting along without an estate manager. They agree that she's a clever woman, though proud and vain, and foolish to think she can run the farm alone.

 Gabriel and the maltster discuss how things have changed over the years at Norcombe. When Gabriel learns that the men have been criticizing Bathsheba, he sternly defends her, thumping his big fist on the table.

THE LETTER

 Boldwood gives Gabriel the letter. It is from Fanny. She returns Gabriel's shilling, thanks him, and says that she is about to marry Troy. She asks him to keep this a secret, but Gabriel immediately shows the letter to Boldwood. ❍ What does Fanny's letter reveal about her character? Do you think Gabriel is right to show Boldwood the letter?

Boldwood takes this opportunity to ask Gabriel if he recognized the handwriting on the envelope that contained the valentine, and he learns that it is Bathsheba's.

Chapter 16 *All Saints' and All Souls*

◆ Troy waits at All Saints' church for Fanny.
◆ She arrives too late and Troy leaves angrily.

Time is a vital element of this chapter, in which Troy waits at the church to marry Fanny. The striking of the clock echoes the clock in the earlier scene outside the barracks. When the bride fails to arrive, there is amusement, then silence, as the tension mounts. A clock with a puppet that emerges to strikes a bell every fifteen minutes seems to make matters worse.

Troy is a proud man and didn't really want to get married in the first place. ❂ How do you think he feels being stood up in public?

Fanny finally enters, anxious, then terrified. She has been waiting at the wrong church. ❂ What are your feelings toward each of them at this point? Is Troy's treatment of Fanny justified?

Time to recap

? From what you've seen so far, circle in one color the words below that describe Troy, and in another those that describe Boldwood. Underline any that describe both.

proud   solitary   impatient   womanizer
obsessive   cruel   serious   careless

? Arrange the objects below in the order in which they appear in the story (Chapters 11–16).

? Write a note from Fanny apologizing to Troy for the mix-up over the wedding.

Take some time off before reading how it's never too late to fall in love (or is it?)

Chapter 17 *In the Market-Place*

◆ Boldwood observes Bathsheba at the market.
◆ Bathsheba regrets having sent the valentine, but can't decide what to do now.

At the market Boldwood sees Bathsheba in a new light. His feelings are very new to him: *Adam had awakened from his deep sleep, and behold! there was Eve.* He has never really noticed a woman in this way before. Despite being a man of 40, he can't even tell whether or not she's beautiful, but already he is half in love.

When Boldwood sees Bathsheba doing business with another farmer, he begins to feel *the injured lover's hell* ❂ Do you think it strange that he falls so quickly and deeply in love? Bathsheba now regrets having sent the valentine, and wonders what to do.

Chapter 18 *Boldwood in Meditation – Regret*

◆ Boldwood described.
◆ Boldwood sees Bathsheba and Gabriel in the fields and decides to speak to her.
◆ He approaches, but cannot bring himself to speak.

Boldwood paces up and down in his stables, like a monk meditating in a cloister. We are told that his apparent stillness of character *may have been the perfect balance of enormous antagonistic forces .... His equilibrium* [balance] *disturbed, he was in extremity at once.* In other words he seems solid, but is in fact unstable.

It is now early spring, when *The vegetable world begins to move and the saps to rise.* Gabriel and Bathsheba are getting sheep who have lost their lambs to adopt motherless lambs. This peaceful work scene contrasts with Boldwood's torment. There is also a comparison between human love and the way in which the sheep are persuaded to "love" new lambs.

❂ Read the second-to-last paragraph. Hardy says that Bathsheba behaves like a flirt but isn't one. Is this possible? Is the chapter's final sentence pessimistic? Why?

Chapter 19 *The Sheep-Washing – The Offer*

◆ Boldwood calls on Bathsheba and is told she is at the sheep washing.
◆ He finds her. She walks away. He follows and proposes.
◆ She says she must have time to think.

Boldwood is deeply in love. The lack of opportunity to get to know her means he idealizes her all the more.
❍ Have you ever idealized someone in this way?

It is now the end of May. The third paragraph gives a beautiful description of nature coming into bloom – the leaves *new, soft, and moist*, and three cuckoos calling (perhaps symbolizing Bathsheba's three lovers).

Boldwood, still *meditating* (deep in thought), hardly notices nature all around him. He goes to the sheep-washing, where Bathsheba is supervising her men. Gabriel is seen thrusting the sheep into the water (for their own good) and helping them out of it. ❍ On one level he's just doing his job, but how might this also reflect his character?

Boldwood, *with solemn simplicity*, tells Bathsheba of his feelings and asks her to marry him. He says he has changed from the confirmed bachelor he once was. His feelings spill out, but Bathsheba seems struck dumb, until she finally confesses to her *thoughtlessness*. He offers her a life of ease in which she *shall never have so much as to look out of doors at haymaking.* ❍ How much will this appeal to her? Bathsheba does not absolutely reject Boldwood. ❍ Which do you think she feels most—pity, guilt, or attraction?

Chapter 20 *Perplexity–Grinding the Shears–A Quarrel*

◆ Bathsheba considers whether she should marry Boldwood.
◆ She goes to Gabriel to find out the men's opinion of her.
◆ She invites Gabriel's opinion of her conduct. He gives it and she fires him.

BATHSHEBA CONSIDERS

Bathsheba realizes that many women would jump at the chance to marry Boldwood. Hardy assumes that most women want to marry. ❂ Why? Think carefully about his comment on the motives for marriage in men and women. ❂ Does Bathsheba owe it to Boldwood to marry him?

SHARPENING THE SHEARS

Bathsheba goes to see Gabriel where he is sharpening sheep shears. Hardy compares this to the sharpening of swords before a battle. Keep this in mind when you later consider Sergeant Troy; both he and Gabriel are craftsmen with a blade. In fact, there is a battle about to take place between Gabriel and Bathsheba.

Gabriel refuses to lie for Bathsheba and offers his opinion on her conduct. She reluctantly asks for it and is proudly angry at his disapproval. ❂ What mistake does Gabriel make in then saying that he thought this reprimand would do her good? Bathsheba becomes spiteful, Gabriel gives his opinion more forcefully, and Bathsheba dismisses him. ❂ What do you think really angers Bathsheba?

Chapter 21 *Trouble in the Fold – A Message*

◆ Bathsheba's sheep get into a field of clover and are in danger of dying from bloating.
◆ Bathsheba sends for Gabriel, who won't come unless asked politely.
◆ She swallows her pride, and he cures the sheep.
◆ She asks him to stay on and he accepts.

Bathsheba faces another dilemma. Her sheep have gotten into some clover and are "blasted" – bloated, doomed unless operated on immediately. Only Gabriel has the skill to pierce their stomachs to release the gas without killing them. It hurts Bathsheba's pride to ask for his help, but she sends a message ordering him to come. He refuses to come unless asked politely. ❂ Is he right to do this? What if Bathsheba lets the sheep die?

Bathsheba gives in. Gabriel comes, and saves almost all the sheep, lancing them with the skill of a surgeon.

Compare his skill with that shown by Troy later in the book.

The chapter ends happily. ✪ How has the incident featured in Bathsheba's personal development? Has Gabriel learned by it as well?

Chapter 22 *The Great Barn and the Sheep-Shearers*

◆ Comments on Gabriel's position and on the time of year.
◆ Description of the shearing barn and the shearing in progress.
◆ Bathsheba times Gabriel shearing a sheep.
◆ Boldwood arrives and departs with Bathsheba.
◆ The rustics discuss Bathsheba and Boldwood, and the shearing supper to come.

It is the first day of June and nature is in its prime, in accord with the lively, positive mood of the chapter, over which a shadow is cast only by Boldwood's arrival.

Hardy describes the ancient shearing barn with the eye of an architect. He gives us a sense of its impressive age and *functional continuity* (for example, it's always been used for the same thing), and compares it favorably with most churches. This leads to a discussion of the way things change more slowly in the country than the city: *The citizen's* THEN *is the rustic's* NOW. ✪ Do you think this is still true? Why does Hardy like the idea of things staying the same?

Bathsheba watches the men shearing, particularly to make sure that no animal is injured. We see Gabriel's skill. He is quietly happy while Bathsheba is standing close by and watching him, but he doesn't allow her presence to distract him from his work. Hardy blames *heartless circumstances* for interrupting Gabriel's happiness with the arrival of Boldwood, which causes him to cut one of the sheep.

Gabriel now thinks he made an absurd mistake in lecturing Bathsheba about Boldwood. He thinks that she really does care for Boldwood. ✪ Does it seem likely at this point that she will marry Boldwood?

Chapter 26 *Scene on the Verge of the Hay-Mead*

◆ Troy flatters and charms Bathsheba at the haymaking.
◆ He gives her his watch, then takes it back again.

Troy has come to make hay, for fun, on Bathsheba's farm. Unlike the real workers, Troy can break off and spend time seducing Bathsheba.

 Follow Troy's technique and the stages of Bathsheba's succumbing to it. ❍ Would you fall for it? Or try it yourself? Troy presents himself as a simple, honest man who merely tells the truth about her beauty and who is her helpless victim. When she comes close to admitting that she is *fascinating*, Troy knows that she has given in to him: *Capitulation – that was the purport of the simple reply.*

Hardy compares him to the devil in paradise. It is clever of Troy to accuse Bathsheba of taking away his *one little ewe-lamb of pleasure*. This phrase refers to the Bible story of King David, who sends Uriah to his death so that he can have his wife. David is accused of being like a rich man who steals a poor man's only sheep. Uriah's wife is called Bathsheba.

Troy declares that he loves Bathsheba, and impulsively makes her a present of his watch, only to take it back again. Compare his watch with Gabriel's (described in Chapter 1).

Chapter 27 *Hiving the Bees*

Troy helps Bathsheba get a swarm of bees into a hive.
Bathsheba agrees to let Troy show her his swordplay.

...sheba is in her garden, about to try to get a swarm of bees ...a hive. Troy comes along and insists on helping her. ...iming is good; she finds it difficult on her own, and ...one else is getting in the hay. Troy dresses up in the ...eeping outfit, and Bathsheba cannot help laughing at him, ...urther dropping her defenses. It becomes almost a game. ...happy to play at rural tasks that are part of the ...ood of real farm workers.

STYLE AND LANGUAGE

The sheep newly shorn by Gabriel are compared to *Aphrodite rising from the foam*. This is one of many references to mythology in the book. Aphrodite is the Greek name for the goddess of love, Venus, born from the sea. Bathsheba is several times compared to her in the book. ❍ If the sheep are being linked to Bathsheba, what might this suggest about her relationship with Gabriel? (The word 'Baa-thsheba' may act as a little memory-jogger!)

Chapter 23 *Eventide – A Second Declaration*

◆ The shearing supper begins.
◆ Bathsheba sings, accompanied by Gabriel and Boldwood.
◆ Bathsheba gives Boldwood some encouragement.

All gather for the shearing supper at Bathsheba's house. Bathsheba is like a queen graciously presiding over her subjects. ❍ What point is made about her position by her end of the table being *thrust over the parlour window*, while the workers' end is outside? And by Gabriel having to give up his place for Boldwood?

The scene is harmonious and pleasant. When the singing begins, the songs are about love. Bathsheba is persuaded to sing. If you have read the whole book, you will understand the ironic significance of the song she chooses. She is accompanied by Gabriel and Boldwood. The trio represents the way their three lives are intertwined.

Bathsheba treats Boldwood *graciously, almost tenderly*. He is encouraged, although she has promised nothing. ❍ What do you think of her behavior?

Review and consider

? Who feels what, and for whom? Make a Mind Map of each character's feelings. Link the Mind Maps to show the personal connections or write each character's name in a separate circle, along with that character's feelings, and add lines to show who those feelings relate to. Here are some words to help you:

anger   hurt   pride   longing   guilt   respect
devotion   love   gratitude   jealousy   sadness

?   Write a caption for each of the pictures below explaining its significance in the story.

now take a break before we meet Troy

Chapter 24 *The Same Night–The Fir Plantation*

◆ Bathsheba makes her nightly tour of the farm.
◆ She meets a stranger, Troy, and her dress gets caught on his spur.
◆ She is confused by his flattery.
◆ Freed, she runs home and finds out about him from Liddy.

At the darkest part of her nightly tour, Bathsheba bumps into a stranger, and the hem of her long dress snags on his spur. Their opening conversation is full of significance. He says, *"We have got hitched together somehow, I think."* This entanglement of spur and dress is the start of an emotional entanglement. His lines, *"Are you a woman?"* and *"I am a man"* suggest an entirely sexual attraction.

Troy flatters her shamelessly, telling her almost at once how beautiful she is. ✪ Why do you think she feels confused? Later

---

she wonders if he has insulted her. Do you think he has Bathsheba learns from Liddy that Troy is *a gay man,* m man who lives for pleasure. Nonetheless, he is clever, educated, and the son of a doctor.

STYLE AND LANGUAGE

Hardy says of Troy: *His sudden appearance was to what the sound of a trumpet is to silence.* ✪ What does this give of his appearance and character? B Troy's shadows are *distorted and mangled.* What make us expect?

Chapter 25 *The New Acquaintance D*

◆ Troy's attitude to life and women described
◆ Bathsheba finds Troy helping with her hay

Unlike Gabriel, who has the farmer's f the seasons, and who learns from the the future, Troy lives almost entirely in the *the past was yesterday; the future, to-morr after.* ✪ Consider the advantages of these Which is more exciting? Which is less lik cause damage?

Troy is not an evil man, but he ha He is *moderately truthful towards* in lying to women, especially in flatter to his view that *in dealing with woma alternative to flattery was cursing and* ✪ Hardy says that women are very e you agree?

STYLE AND LANGUAG

At the end of the chapter, Troy is Compare this with the red seal o does red usually mean? What sho

Bat
into
His
ever
beek
thus
Troy
liveli

❂ Do you think that when Troy mentions the sword exercise, he is already thinking of it as a way to impress Bathsheba? She agrees to meet him, without Liddy, in order to see it.

Chapter 28 *The Hollow amid the Ferns*

◆ Bathsheba goes to meet Troy in a secluded place.
◆ He shows off his swordplay. She is dazzled and excited.
◆ He kisses her, and she is overcome with emotion.

This famous chapter is full of sexual symbolism. For example when Bathsheba walks into the ferns to meet Troy, she feels *their soft, feathery arms caressing her up to her shoulders.* She changes her mind, dimly aware of the danger, and almost goes home, but then sees the *dim spot of artificial red* that is Troy.

Troy's sword, which *gleamed a sort of greeting, like a living thing,* is a symbol of his masculinity. The main part of his demonstration involves Bathsheba in being completely passive, because for safety, she must remain motionless. There is excitement in her role as his *antagonist*, with his sword whirring around her, enclosing her in *a firmament of light, and of sharp hisses, resembling a sky-full of meteors close at hand.*

Troy is superbly skilled. The cutting off of a lock of her hair is pure showmanship. It becomes significant later, when she finds that he already carries a lock from another lover. The spearing of the caterpillar amazes her. When he kisses her, she is too dazed to resist. ❂ Do you admire Troy? Is Bathsheba being a fool?

Chapter 29 *Particulars of a Twilight Walk*

◆ Gabriel wants to warn Bathsheba against Troy. She denies involvement with Boldwood and defends Troy.
◆ Bathsheba tries to dismiss Gabriel again, but he won't go.
◆ Gabriel sees Troy approaching.

Bathsheba now loves Troy *in the way that only self-reliant women love when they abandon their self-reliance.* She is a strong woman who has given all her power to Troy. ❂ Do you think women should be at all reliant on men?

49

Gabriel sees her infatuation and decides he must warn her against Troy and argue in favor of Boldwood. He warns her that there are *bad characters about* and is about to use this to introduce the subject of Troy, when he realizes, with a tact that he seems to be learning now, that this would be clumsy. Instead, he speaks of Boldwood, and Bathsheba denies any attachment to him.

❂ Do you think there is any hope of his persuading Bathsheba to be wary of Troy? Why does the idea of Troy slipping into church by a side door seem to Gabriel *like the thirteenth stroke of a crazy clock?* Why does Bathsheba believe Troy? How does Gabriel disprove it?

With great unselfishness, Gabriel tries to persuade Bathsheba to marry Boldwood. Bathsheba tries to dismiss Gabriel again, but this time he stands up for himself and refuses to take her seriously.

Chapter 30 *Hot Cheeks and Tearful Eyes*

◆ Bathsheba writes to Boldwood to say that she cannot marry him.
◆ Bathsheba denies loving Troy, then confesses it to Liddy.
◆ Liddy stands up for herself when Bathsheba rages at her, then they make up.

Bathsheba is in emotional turmoil. She tells her servants she hates Troy, then threatens to dismiss any of them who say a word against him. She confides in Liddy, but then threatens her with dismissal if she betrays her secret, so that Liddy threatens to leave: *"I don't see that I deserve to be put upon and stormed at for nothing!"* The two women are tearfully reconciled.

What do you know? What do you think?

? Begin a Mind Map of the developing relationship between Troy and Bathsheba. What are the key points so far?

? Draw your answers to the following questions in the boxes below. You don't have to be an artist – just create an image that *you* can recognize.

- On what does Bathsheba's dress get caught among the dark firs (Chapter 24)?
- What rural activity does Troy help Bathsheba with in her garden (Chapter 27)?
- With what does Troy impress Bathsheba in the "hollow amid the ferns" (Chapter 28)?
- What does Troy spear without hurting Bathsheba (Chapter 28)?

? Divide a sheet of paper into three columns, headed **Gabriel**, **Boldwood,** and **Troy**. List each man's "selling points" as a partner for Bathsheba, or Mind Map them.

Bathsheba's about to try a change of scene – so why don't you?

Chapter 31 *Blame – Fury*

- Bathsheba tries to avoid Boldwood, but meets him out walking.
- He begs her to have pity for him in his love for her.
- She says she regrets the valentine, but insists that she promised Boldwood nothing.
- She admits that she loves Troy, and Boldwood vows revenge on him.

It is now midsummer. Bathsheba sets off to visit Liddy's sister, but only to avoid Boldwood. When she accidentally meets him, he is downcast and desperate; he protests his love – *strong as death*, and begs her to take pity on him. He says, "*I am beyond myself about this, and am mad.*" ❂ How do you feel about this once self-sufficient man reduced to what he calls *that low, lowest stage* and *weak, idle drivelling*? How would you feel if someone who wanted to go out with you begged this way?

Bathsheba says she regrets having sent the valentine, but she still defends herself: "*How was I to know that what is a pastime to all other men was death to you?*" If you know how the story unfolds, you will see the irony in this. ❂ Do you think she really believes that all other men treat love lightly (as a pastime)? Is there a man in the novel who doesn't?

CONFESSION AND CURSE

Bathsheba is basically honest and cannot deny that she loves Troy or that she has kissed him. Boldwood is in a fury of jealous pain. He curses Troy and vows revenge on him. From here on, this threat hangs over the story. Bathsheba takes it seriously, and rightly so.

STYLE AND LANGUAGE

When Boldwood has gone, Bathsheba gazes at the *indecisive and palpitating stars*: even the heavens, usually seen as a symbol of constancy, now seem to be unreliable.

Chapter 32 *Night – Horses tramping*

◆ Maryann is awakened in the night by what seems to be a horse thief.
◆ Gabriel and Coggan set out in pursuit, only to find it is Bathsheba.
◆ We learn that Bathsheba has decided to give Troy up, and has been on her way to Bath to tell him.

 It is night, and Maryann thinks a horse has been stolen by a gypsy. Gabriel and Jan Coggan borrow two of Boldwood's horses and ride in pursuit, expertly tracking the "thief" in the darkness. They are surprised when they catch up with Bathsheba. ✪ Why doesn't it even occur to them that it might be her?

 STYLE AND LANGUAGE

In order to keep up the suspense, Hardy lets us think, like Gabriel and Coggan, that they are tracking a thief. This means that the last part of the chapter has to explain what Bathsheba was doing. ✪ Does this work? Did you suspect the truth?

Chapter 33 *In the Sun – A Harbinger*

◆ Bathsheba is away for two weeks during harvesttime.
◆ Cain Ball brings news that he has seen Bathsheba and Troy together in Bath.

It is a hot harvesttime. For the first time, Bathsheba neglects her farm by being away at this busy time. We are led to expect bad news by Maryann reporting a broken door key, perhaps the same one that Bathsheba and Liddy used in the fortune-telling game.

Cain Ball, Gabriel's young assistant, comes running with the news that he has seen Bathsheba and Troy arm in arm in Bath. At first he can't get the story out because he has swallowed some food the wrong way. This keeps the suspense up, and provides a sort of black humor. It is one of the few times in the novel when Gabriel shows impatience.

Chapter 34 *Home again – A Trickster*

◆ Bathsheba returns and Boldwood goes to visit her to apologize and beg her forgiveness.
◆ Troy appears and Boldwood confronts him, then offers him money to wed Fanny.
◆ Bathsheba appears and speaks fondly to Troy.
◆ Boldwood nearly kills Troy, but in the end offers him money to wed Bathsheba.
◆ Troy reveals that he has already married her.

This chapter shows Troy and Boldwood at their worst, and shows the worst aspects of love. Boldwood has stooped to offering Troy money to marry Fanny. Perhaps he is in part doing this for Fanny's sake, but it is mostly to get Troy away from Bathsheba.

Troy tells Boldwood, *"I love Fanny best now. ... But Bathsh – Miss Everdene inflamed me, and displaced Fanny for a time. It is over now."* ❂ How far do you think he is telling the truth, and how far just playing with Boldwood? Certainly it seems to end up being the truth.

Bathsheba appears and speaks fondly to Troy, causing Boldwood to suffer agonies of jealousy. When Bathsheba is gone, he nearly kills Troy. He feels even worse when Troy says that only he can save Bathsheba by marrying her. Troy is implying that he has already been to bed with Bathsheba.

❂ Do you feel sorry for Boldwood when he switches to offering Troy money to marry Bathsheba? Troy seems to enjoy torturing Boldwood, saying that he doesn't wish to *"... secure her in any new way."* To "secure her" means to make her his. ❂ What is he saying, and why? When Troy reveals that he has already married Bathsheba and continues to taunt Boldwood, the older man again vows revenge. ❂ Would Boldwood be justified in killing Troy?

Chapter 35 *At an Upper Window*

◆ Gabriel and Coggan learn that Bathsheba has married Troy. Gabriel is deeply grieved.
◆ Troy throws them a coin.
◆ Boldwood is seen riding past.

It is early in the morning when Gabriel and Coggan encounter Troy leaning from Bathsheba's bedroom window. It can only mean that Troy and Bathsheba are married. This is *an unutterable grief* to Gabriel. It is also surprising, since it is not like Bathsheba to do anything in secret.

Troy talks about modernizing the house. ❂ Keeping in mind Hardy's comments on the ancient shearing barn (Chapter 22), what does Troy's attitude suggest? Why does Coggan advise Gabriel not to make his dislike of Troy too obvious?

The chapter ends with a glimpse of Boldwood. We see *in the steadiness of this agonized man an expression deeper than a cry.* ❖ From this line, how might we expect him to behave now?

Chapter 36 *Wealth in Jeopardy – The Revel*

◆ The harvest supper is held. Gabriel is absent.
◆ Gabriel realizes that a storm is coming and that the grain must be protected.
◆ Troy ignores Gabriel and gets the men drunk.
◆ Gabriel sets to work on the grain on his own.

Trouble is brewing. The harvest supper is in process, presided over by Bathsheba and Troy. (He is *lolling beside her.*) Gabriel can tell from signs in nature – the rooks (birds), the sheep, the horses, and the sky (see the second paragraph) – that a storm is probably on its way. He sends a message to Troy, who is now in charge, that the hay needs to be covered to protect it. Troy ignores him, then sends the women home and gets all the men drunk on brandy.

Note the difference in attitude between Troy and Gabriel. Note, too, the way Troy corrupts the men, who are not used to strong drink. Bathsheba tries to stop him, but to no avail. ❖ Troy behaves irresponsibly, but is there anything you could say in his defense?

Hardy personifies nature as *the Great Mother.* She sends Gabriel three messages:

He takes these as signs that the storm is coming, but he is finally convinced by the behavior of his sheep.

Finding that the men are in a drunken stupor, Gabriel gets the necessary tools and sets to work.

 STYLE AND LANGUAGE

Read the last paragraph of the chapter. Notice how the description of natural things reflects the mood and suggests the danger to come. Find the lines that compare the night to a dying person.

Chapter 37 *The Storm – The Two Together*

◆ Gabriel works to protect the grain.
◆ Bathsheba joins him and they work together through the storm.
◆ Bathsheba confides in Gabriel that she married Troy out of jealousy.
◆ Bathsheba gives Gabriel heartfelt thanks.

This chapter shows the power of nature, and Gabriel's knowledge, ability, and courage in battling against it. In Chapter 6 he saved Bathsheba's hay from fire, and now he saves the grain from water. Now, as then, he knows what to do; note the way he improvises a lightning conductor that prevents him and Bathsheba from being struck by lightning.

Bathsheba is disappointed in Troy, who *promised that the grain should be seen to*. He has let her down badly, whereas Gabriel is as reliable as ever. She wonders why no one else is helping, and then realizes that this, too, is Troy's fault.

BATHSHEBA CONFIDES IN GABRIEL

Brought closer to Gabriel by the shared work and danger, Bathsheba confides why she married Troy in Bath. In the past she has angrily claimed to be indifferent to what Gabriel thinks of her. Now she says that she cares for his good opinion. She tells him that Troy manipulated her into becoming his by saying he'd never seen a more beautiful woman:

"... his constancy could not be counted on unless I at once became his."

 Gabriel is struck by the feminine *contradictoriness* that makes Bathsheba speak more warmly to him now that she is married when one might normally expect the opposite. ✪ What detail at the end of the chapter reflects this view of women?

✏ STYLE AND LANGUAGE

Reread the paragraph describing the storm at its peak, beginning, *Heaven opened then.* Notice the skeleton shapes, the *undulating snakes of green*, and the *shout* that is the clap of thunder. ✪ What overall impression is made? This is a good example of setting (location, weather, and so on), reflecting what is happening with the characters.

Chapter 38 *Rain – One Solitary Meets Another*

◆ Gabriel finishes protecting Bathsheba's grain as it begins to rain heavily.
◆ Troy and the men emerge from the barn.
◆ Gabriel meets Boldwood, who has neglected his grain.
◆ Boldwood confides in Gabriel about his feelings for Bathsheba.

We see more of the power of nature, as the snarling wind rocks the trees and the downfall begins. Gabriel is *drenched, weary and sad*, though *cheered by success in a good cause.* He makes a strong contrast to Troy and the men shuffling home after their drunken sleep.

Gabriel meets Boldwood, who seems distracted. Gabriel is shocked to find that Boldwood has forgotten to have his fields protected so that now his grain will have been ruined. We see the damage that Boldwood's obsessive love for Bathsheba has done. A few months earlier, Boldwood's neglecting his farm would have been *as preposterous an idea as a sailor forgetting he was in a ship.* Almost as uncharacteristic is the way Boldwood suddenly tells Gabriel of his deep misery as he is normally so reserved.

✪ Read the last paragraph. What image reminds us that Boldwood is not very good at pretending?

Test your memory and understanding

?   Troy sums up the exchange between him and Boldwood (Chapter 34) in these words: *"Fifty pounds to marry Fanny. Good. Twenty-one pounds not to marry Fanny, but Bathsheba. Good. Finale: already Bathsheba's husband."* What does he mean? What does he intend by his words? If you can't remember, check the chapter.

?   What part does nature play in Chapters 36 and 37? Make a Mini Mind Map. Clues: Gabriel's three messages, his sheep, the grain fields.

?   Sum up in your own words (or in pictures) what Gabriel, Bathsheba, and Troy are doing during the storm.

find out what has happened to Fanny – but first take a break

Chapter 39   *Coming Home – A Cry*

◆ On the way back from market, Troy tells Bathsheba about his gambling losses.

◆ They meet Fanny Robin, and Troy gives her money.

It is now October, and Troy and Bathsheba are traveling home from the market. Always a dandy, Troy is wearing an unusually fashionable farmer's suit. He aims light flicks of the whip at the horse *as a recreation*, suggesting his casual cruelty.

Troy is complaining that the rain has spoiled his chances of winning money at the horse races. Remember the significance of rain in the previous chapter and compare it with this. Troy's gambling can be compared with Bathsheba's willingness to put herself in the hands of chance – or fate – when she tossed the hymnal to decide who to send the valentine to. ○ What does she think of Troy's betting now? (Remember, too, that it's her money!)

Troy and Bathsheba meet a poor woman on the road. Typically, Hardy does not tell us at first that it's Fanny Robin. Troy sends Bathsheba on so that he can speak to Fanny.
❂ Does it seem to you that he cares about Fanny? Why does he say, *I am a brute?*

Chapter 40 *On Casterbridge Highway*

◆ Fanny tries to reach Casterbridge.
◆ She is helped by a dog.

This chapter presents a sad, pathetic portrayal of Fanny Robin. Sick, exhausted, and – as we later discover – pregnant, she struggles to drag herself the last two miles to Casterbridge, where she is supposed to meet Troy. It is night, and the mournful barking of a fox sets the mood.

She is helped temporarily by some crutches that she makes for herself and then by tricking herself into thinking that she doesn't have so far to go. Finally, a large dog appears and helps her to get to the Union (the workhouse, where she will get food and shelter).

The dog is a symbol of the kind of simple loyalty that poor Fanny has not found in humanity, especially in Troy. **Ironically**, the dog is stoned away by a man at the workhouse. (The irony lies in the cruel twist of fate: The man cannot know that the dog, in fact, deserves a reward.)

Chapter 41 *Suspicion – Fanny is Sent For*

◆ Troy asks Bathsheba for money and refuses to tell her what it's for.
◆ Bathsheba sees a lock of hair in Troy's watch. He admits that it belongs to a woman he was going to marry and that she is the one they met on the road.
◆ Joseph brings news that Fanny is dead, and Bathsheba sends him to bring back her body.
◆ Bathsheba becomes increasingly suspicious that Fanny was Troy's lover.

Troy is seen lying to Bathsheba, but only half-heartedly. He allows her to think that he needs the money for the races, and she tries to charm him into staying at home. Then he admits that the money is for something else, but won't say what, becoming angry when Bathsheba tries to assert her right to know.

When Bathsheba complains that her romance with him has ended, he replies, *"All romances end at marriage."* ✪ Do you think he believes this, or is he just trying to hurt her?

THE LOCK OF HAIR

Bathsheba relents and gives Troy the money, but then a new source of conflict arises: the lock of hair. We see how much Bathsheba has changed and how little she now expects of life in her bitter outburst: *"Ah! once I felt I could be content with nothing less than the highest homage from the husband I should choose. Now, anything short of cruelty will content me."*

Note the line, *Diana was the goddess whom Bathsheba instinctively adored.* Here, as before, Bathsheba is compared to a goddess, Diana, who was the proud and independent virgin huntress. Bathsheba wishes she had stayed unmarried, her own mistress.

FANNY'S DEATH REPORTED

Hardy shows us what Bathsheba sees as a pantomime in the distance: Boldwood coming up the road, Boldwood meeting Gabriel, the two men in earnest conversation, and then speaking to Joseph Poorgrass. Joseph then brings her the news that Fanny is dead.

At first Bathsheba responds with kindness and generosity, instructing Joseph to bring Fanny back in a pretty wagon heaped with evergreens and flowers. However, she turns pale and becomes restless as she begins to suspect the awful truth—that Fanny was Troy's lover. She asks Joseph the color of Fanny's hair, and whose sweetheart she was. When Liddy confirms that Fanny's hair was golden, the color of the hair in Troy's locket, Bathsheba is almost certain.

Chapter 42 *Joseph and his Burden – Buck's Head*

◆ Joseph brings back Fanny's body from Casterbridge Unionhouse.

◆ He is unnerved by having to drive the body alone through the gloomy fog.

◆ He goes into the Buck's Head and gets drunk with Jan Coggan and Mark Clark.

◆ Gabriel finds him there, tells him off, and then takes charge of the wagon himself.

◆ When Gabriel reaches Weatherbury, Parson Thirdly says that the funeral must now be on the next day.

◆ Gabriel takes the wagon to Bathsheba's house, and Bathsheba insists that the coffin be brought in for the night.

STYLE AND LANGUAGE

Hardy begins the chapter using a technique that should now be very familiar to you: the description of a scene with only its physical details and no explanation of them. Here he focuses on the strangeness of a door perched three or four feet above ground level. We discover its purpose when Joseph pulls the wagon up beneath it and Fanny's coffin is laid in place.

This chapter is also notable for the wonderful way in which Hardy uses the setting of the foggy fall woods to create atmosphere. The *scrolls of mist* creep in from the sea in a rather menacing way. They are *the silent workings of an invisible hand*. The *dead silence* is broken only by the occasional branch falling from a tree and rapping on the coffin. ❂ What might this sound make a nervous man like Joseph imagine? It is no wonder that he begins to yearn for company.

The gloom gives way to some rather black comedy when Joseph comes to a pub and goes in to raise his spirits. There he, Coggan, and Mark Clark proceed to get so drunk that Joseph begins to see everything "two by two" as if he were *some holy man living in the times of King Noah and entering into the ark*. ❂ What do you think of Coggan's argument that Joseph may as well stay and

61

drink, because hurrying won't bring the dead woman back to life and of his arguments in favor of drinking generally ("*A man's twice the man afterwards ...*")?

Gabriel, as ever, assumes responsibility and takes the coffin to Weatherbury himself, only to be told by Parson Thirdly that it's now too late for the funeral to take place that day. He tries to persuade Bathsheba to allow the coffin to remain on the wagon for the night, but she won't hear of it, insisting that the coffin be brought into the house. ❍ Do you agree with Bathsheba that it would be unkind to leave it outside? What further insight does this give us into Bathsheba's character?

Gabriel has done his best to protect Bathsheba, but it seems that circumstances, or fate, are mocking him. Despite his efforts, *the very worst event that could in any way have happened in connection with the burial* has now happened: Bathsheba is going to be spending the night under the same roof as her husband's dead lover!

Gabriel does the one thing he can now do to help. He rubs out the words ... *and child* from the coffin lid. ❍ Why does he do this?

Chapter 43 *Fanny's Revenge*

◆ Bathsheba dismisses Liddy, saying that she will sit up and wait for Troy to come home herself.
◆ Before Liddy goes, she tells Bathsheba of the rumor that Fanny died giving birth.
◆ Tormented, Bathsheba goes to ask Gabriel if this is true, but cannot bring herself to disturb him.
◆ Bathsheba goes home, opens the coffin herself, and discovers Fanny's baby there.
◆ Troy comes in, kisses Fanny's dead lips, and pushes Bathsheba away.
◆ Bathsheba flees into the night.

The story now reaches a dramatic climax. Liddy offers to wait up for Troy, but Bathsheba sends her to bed. Liddy goes, but not before giving Bathsheba fresh cause for anxiety. She whispers to her the rumor that Fanny died giving birth to a baby. Almost convinced that Fanny was Troy's lover, Bathsheba must now cope with the possibility that Fanny has died giving birth to Troy's child!

Tormented by a mixture of grief, loneliness, and anxiety, and yet determined to know the truth, Bathsheba resolves to speak to the one person she feels can give her emotional support and advice: Gabriel. Notice the line, *What a way Oak had, she thought, of enduring things.* This is a comment both on his character and on her respect for it.

She sees Gabriel through the window of his house and yet somehow cannot bring herself to attract his attention and reveal her misery to him. Perhaps the contrast between the apparent peace and contentment in his house, and the agitation in her own heart are too much for her. She goes home, still suffering. Try to picture her. Hardy gives us a vivid image: *She locked her fingers, threw back her head, and strained her hot hands rigidly across her forehead.* Try copying her gesture yourself to get a physical picture of how she is feeling and to fix the image in your memory.

OPENING THE COFFIN

Bathsheba is so tortured by uncertainty that she resolves to open the coffin and see its contents with her own eyes. Soon she stands, *quivering with emotion, a mist before her eyes, and an excruciating pulsation in her brain*, looking at the open coffin. ❂ How do you judge her determination *to know the worst?* Is she being brave or stupid?

Finally, we see Fanny's golden hair, and Bathsheba now has little doubt that Fanny had been the owner of the lock of hair treasured by Troy. Bathsheba considers suicide, but decides against it. She is torn between jealous hatred and pity for Fanny, but is calmed a little by praying, and then laying flowers around Fanny's head.

The scene reaches its terrible climax when Troy walks in and gradually realizes what has happened. Remember that up until now he has not known of Fanny's death. He is shocked and so affected by *clashes of feeling* that for the first time we see this man of action motionless and at a loss about what to do. He sinks forward, his face showing *illimitable sadness,* and kisses Fanny. ✪ What do you feel about Troy at this moment? Do you sympathize with his loss?

Bathsheba tries desperately to make Troy kiss her. For a moment he is bewildered by this proof that all women are *alike at heart* in their rivalry for a man's affections. Nonetheless, he rejects Bathsheba, although he admits to having been *a bad, black-hearted man.*

✪ How do you respond to Troy's declaration of love for Fanny? Is this genuine? Or is it just that he's the kind of man who only wants what he can't have and finds it easier to be loyal to a dead woman than a living one?

Chapter 44 *Under a Tree – Reaction*

◆ Bathsheba spends the night in the woods.
◆ Liddy finds her and they return home.
◆ Bathsheba settles down with Liddy in the attic.

Bathsheba disappears into the night, not knowing or caring where she's going. The place she finds herself in seems to be the same *hollow amid the ferns* where Troy demonstrated his swordplay to her in the earliest days of their love affair (Chapter 28). The ferns are *now withering fast,* as is her relationship with Troy.

Remember that on more than one occasion Hardy has likened Bathsheba to the goddess Diana, a nature goddess, and pointed out that she is a country girl at heart. No wonder, then, that in her hour of need she finds comfort in nature. In the morning she feels calmer. The description of the simple, innocent wildlife is also refreshing to the reader after the wild, emotional scenes of the last chapter. The passing plowboy also represents innocence. When Bathsheba shakes off the fall leaves from her dress and they *flutter away in the breeze thus created, "like ghosts from an enchanter fleeing"* (from Shelley's poem, "Ode to the West Wind"), some of the ghosts of the previous night leave her too.

STYLE AND LANGUAGE

Some of Hardy's best descriptions are of nature. Here we see nature as beauty, *the beautiful yellowing ferns with their feathery arms*, and in a more sinister light, as *malignant* [evil], *poisonous*. There is a profusion of fungi (toadstools) growing on rotting leaves and tree stumps. In the red marks on some of them we see again Hardy's use of this color to suggest danger, as in Troy's coat and the seal on the valentine, and again in the blood-red sun at the end of the chapter.

The hollow seems to be *a nursery of pestilences small and great, in the immediate neighbourhood of comfort and health.* (A pestilence is a disease.) Bathsheba now sees the danger she was unaware of when first courted there by Troy.

NEW RESOLVE

Bathsheba seems to have found new strength. She decides that *it is only women with no pride in them who run away from their husbands*, and that it is better to die of a husband's ill treatment than to run away. ✪ What do you think of this attitude? Note that in Hardy's own time, many people would have agreed with her.

Bathsheba launches into a survival plan: to live in the attic, apart from Troy. She gives Liddy a list of very gloomy books to bring her and then changes her mind and demands more cheerful ones. Despite this, the carefree game of Prisoners' Base played by the young men of the village is in contrast to Bathsheba's situation. It might also suggest that Bathsheba is a prisoner in her own home.

Chapter 45 *Troy's Romanticism*

◆ We hear how Troy has spent the last twenty-four hours.
◆ Troy spends all the money he has on an expensive tombstone for Fanny.

The beginning of the chapter goes back in time. First we see, briefly, how Troy has spent the night lying miserably on the bed (while Bathsheba has been in the woods). Then we hear how Fate has *dealt grimly* with him. He has set out to do Fanny some good by taking her the money he has wrung out of Bathsheba, together with some of his own (Hardy adds it up for us). He has arranged to meet her, and has gone off angrily to the races when she has failed to turn up. This is the second time Fanny has failed to turn up to meet him. ○ Can you remember the first? If not, turn back to Chapter 16.

Returning to the present, Hardy describes how Troy goes to buy a tombstone for Fanny. He goes about it *like a child in a nursery*. This seems to suggest that this attempt to do some good in the world is very new to Troy. ○ Does he at other times seem in any way childlike to you?

In familiar style, Hardy describes the sight of Troy carrying a mysterious burden. Only when he arrives at the churchyard, and at Fanny's tomb, *snow-white and shapely* (like her), do we discover that his basket contains flowers and bulbs to plant on the grave. We see Troy in the uncharacteristic role of gardener. Picture him carefully planting around the grave by lantern light.

Hardy says that Troy's deeds are *dictated by a remorseful reaction from previous indifference*. In other words, he feels guilty that he didn't care about Fanny while she was alive. Hardy suggests there is something absurd and ridiculous in what he is now doing. ○ How convincing do you find Troy's apparent regret for letting Fanny down?

Give your brain a helping hand

?   Imagine you're watching a TV version of *Far from the Madding Crowd*. A friend comes in just in time to catch the conversation between Troy and Fanny on the road, at the end of Chapter 39. What key facts would you have to explain for your friend to understand the conversation?

?   Reread Chapter 42, paragraphs 6–8 (*The afternoon ... auburn hair*). Underline or write down the words or phrases that help to create the gloomy, slightly scary atmosphere.

?   How has Troy treated Bathsheba? Add to (or start) your Mind Map of their relationship.

? The items shown in the illustration feature in a documentary about Fanny Robin. What would the voice-over say about each one?

now take a break before Troy's accident at sea

Chapter 46 *The Gurgoyle: its Doings*

◆ Hardy describes the gargoyles on the church.
◆ Heavy rain spouting from a gargoyle washes away the flowers from Fanny's grave.
◆ Troy discovers what has happened, despairs, and leaves the village.
◆ Bathsheba discovers the washed-out grave and replants the flowers.

In this chapter we are reminded that Hardy was once a stonemason and apprentice architect. The chapter begins with his affectionate description of the grotesque gargoyles (old spelling is *gurgoyles*) on the church tower, whose practical task is to funnel rainwater off the roof.

It seems a rather bitter twist of fate that Fanny's grave just happens to be exactly in the path of the water spouting so fiercely from one of these gargoyles after the night's heavy rain. The *persistent torrent* is said to direct *all its vengeance into the grave*. It makes the flowers *move and writhe in their bed*. The

67

bulbs dance *in the boiling mass like ingredients in a cauldron.* It's like something in a horror movie! Hardy's language suggests an almost vicious fate at work in the shape of the gargoyle.

After the night's rain, the morning dawns beautifully clear. Hardy even compares the effect to the work of two Dutch landscape painters. Troy's discovery is in stark contrast. All his work has been destroyed; the flowers and bulbs have all been washed down the path. We can see his reaction in Hardy's description of his facial expression. Try it out for yourself in the mirror. At the very least, it will help fix the incident in your mind. ✪ Does Hardy's description seem accurate?

> *Troy's brow became heavily contracted. He set his teeth closely, and his compressed lips moved as those of one in great pain.*

The two paragraphs beginning *Almost for the first time in his life Troy ... wished himself another man* are important if you want to understand this man's character and how it develops. They are well worth rereading. Notice how his *first critical and trembling* efforts to become a better man have been nipped in the bud. He feels that providence (fate) has scorned him, and he gives up easily and completely.

Compare his attitude to that of Bathsheba, who never quite gives up in this way. When she finds the uprooted flowers, she replants them. Whether or not Hardy is right in thinking that women make better gardeners than men, the contrast between Troy and Bathsheba could not be clearer.

Chapter 47 *Adventures by the Shore*

◆ Troy leaves Weatherbury.
◆ He arrives at the sea and goes for a swim.
◆ He almost drowns, but is picked up by a passing boat.

Troy heads south, *to seek a home in any place on earth save Weatherbury.* Coming over a hill he is met by a view of the sea, presented in one of Hardy's classic descriptions of nature. The language suggests that the scene would appeal to Troy: the *broad steely sea* on which *the sun bristled down.* His hope seems to return, as he is compared to Balboa, the first Spaniard to set eyes on the Pacific. This is in anticipation of Troy's going to America.

Troy goes for a swim. Being a man who likes a challenge, he swims out into the ocean swell and is nearly swept away and drowned. However, he is saved by some passing sailors.

 STYLE AND LANGUAGE

Notice how, in the last paragraph, each lamplight seems *to send a flaming sword deep down into the waves before it.* Troy, the swordsman, is once again in his element, in a man's world.

Chapter 48 *Doubts arise – Doubts linger*

◆ Bathsheba goes to the market and receives the message that Troy has been drowned.

◆ She faints and is carried to an inn by Boldwood.

◆ She is convinced that Troy is still alive, but when given his clothes she begins to think he may really be dead.

◆ She almost burns the lock of Fanny's hair, but then decides to keep it.

Bathsheba sinks into a state of grim resignation to her fate, without hope or anxiety. She thinks Troy will eventually return, that they will be unable to pay the rent on the farm, and that she will become a pauper. Nonetheless, she continues to do business, and it is at the market that she gets the message saying that Troy has been drowned. Try to imagine the mixture of feelings she must have at this point. She faints and is carried to an inn by Boldwood, who tenderly smoothes her dress *as a child might have taken a storm-beaten bird and arranged its ruffled plumes.* (What a contrast to Troy!)

Bathsheba thinks Troy is still alive. Liddy speaks of getting Bathsheba a mourning dress, but Bathsheba says it won't be necessary. ✪ Does this seem like the normal disbelief of bereavement (especially when there is no body), or that Bathsheba intuitively knows the truth?

Examining Troy's clothes, Bathsheba finds his watch and takes out the lock of Fanny's hair. Her decision to keep it in memory of Fanny is both courageous and generous.

Chapter 49 *Oak's Advancement – A Great Hope*

◆ Gabriel becomes the manager of Bathsheba's farm, and then of Boldwood's as well.
◆ Boldwood begins to hope that Bathsheba will one day be his wife.

It is now the beginning of winter. In keeping with the season, Bathsheba is apathetic, as if her life is over. One positive outcome of this is that she promotes Gabriel to the post of manager. Boldwood is similarly inactive, and hires Gabriel to be his manager as well.

There is evidence of change in the other main characters as well. Bathsheba has been persuaded to accept the fact that Troy is dead, at least to the extent of wearing mourning. Boldwood recognizes that suffering has made her *much more considerate than she had formerly been of the feelings of others*. He begins to hope that she will one day be his wife and tries to discover, from Liddy, Bathsheba's feelings about remarriage. He goes away ashamed of having behaved in an underhanded way *for this one time in his life.* ✪ Is this really the first time? Look back to Chapter 34.

Chapter 50 *The Sheep Fair–Troy touches his Wife's Hand*

◆ Bathsheba goes to the sheep fair at Greenhill.
◆ Troy is there, in a traveling show.
◆ Bathsheba watches the show but does not recognize Troy.
◆ Pennyways does, and out of spite gives Bathsheba a note telling her.
◆ Troy manages to steal the note before she reads it.

This is an action-packed chapter, although it begins with a long description of the sheep fair that would appeal to Hardy's city-dwelling readers. They would also enjoy the comedy of the country folk pressing into the tent to see the show.

When Troy realizes that Bathsheba is there, he wants to avoid being recognized. One line is worth memorizing: *Troy was never more clever than when absolutely at his wits' end.* He decides to add to his disguise, and to perform without speaking, relying on his skill as a rider and marksman. We learn that it is on similar skills that he has survived in America.

There is great drama and suspense. We want to know whether Troy will be recognized, and he is, but by Pennyways, not Bathsheba. Pennyways has continued to hold a grudge against his former mistress. Picture the scene where he hands her the note and Troy manages to snatch it away through a slit in the canvas. ❂ How would you show this in a film?

Chapter 51 *Bathsheba talks with her Outrider*

◆ Boldwood accompanies Bathsheba back to Weatherbury and tries to make her promise to marry him in six years.
◆ Bathsheba goes to ask Gabriel's advice.

Boldwood rides beside Bathsheba. She knows she has wronged him in the past and sympathizes deeply with his continuing feelings for her. He mistakes her pity for tenderness and asks once again if she will marry him in six years when she can legally do so if Troy fails to appear. He thinks the time will glide by, and sees himself as Jacob, who has to work *twice seven years* to win Rachel.
❂ What do you think she should do? Is she right to feel responsible for Boldwood's feelings?

She seeks advice from Gabriel, who suggests that she might make Boldwood a *conditional promise*. However, he adds later: *"The real sin, ma'am, in my mind, lies in thinking of ever wedding wi' a man you don't love honest and true."* ❂ Do you agree? Note Bathsheba's *little pang of disappointment* that Gabriel shows no sign that he loves her himself.

Try This

? Read the following article in the *Budmouth Gazette* and underline any inaccuracies:

> A Casterbridge man, Mr. Frederick Troy (28), drowned yesterday swimming at Lulwind Cove. A Mr. Barker, MD, of Budmouth, was witness to the tragedy. Mr. Troy leaves behind a wife, Bathsheba (born Evergreen), and a young son. Though a dedicated farmer, Mr. Troy was, before marriage, a corporal in the King's Infantry. He was a teetotaller, a regular church-goer, and an excellent swordsman. Sadly, however, he was a poor swimmer.

? Add to your Mind Map of the relationship between Troy and Bathsheba.

now leave Bathsheba with her dilemma and take a break

Chapter 52 *Converging Courses*

◆ Boldwood plans a Christmas party.
◆ Bathsheba prepares for the party.
◆ Troy discusses his legal position and plan to return with Pennyways.

The construction of this chapter is interesting. It is divided into seven short scenes in which we see what Bathsheba and her three lovers – Boldwood, Troy, and Gabriel – are all doing while preparations for Boldwood's Christmas party are being made. It is as if four trains are seen heading separately toward a single point; hence the chapter title. ❂ What do you expect to happen when they converge?

In **Scene 1** we see party preparations going on. Boldwood spares no expense, and yet, *Intended gaieties would insist on appearing like solemn grandeurs*. In **Scene 2** Liddy helps Bathsheba dress for the party. Bathsheba is worried that the party is all for her. In **Scene 3** Boldwood nervously dresses, accompanied by a tailor and by Gabriel. Boldwood insensitively tells Gabriel all about his hopes and anxieties concerning Bathsheba. **Scene 4** takes place in a tavern, where Troy is also discussing plans that involve Bathsheba. Pennyways has become a sort of henchman to Troy. Troy intends to go to the party in disguise and confront Bathsheba. ✪ What do you think of his plan?

In **Scene 5** we are back in Bathsheba's room. She is dressing plainly, because she doesn't want to seem as if she is trying to attract Boldwood. She assures Liddy that she has no plans to marry. It is therefore ironic when **Scene 6** shows us Boldwood promising Gabriel a raise because of his new hopes and later contemplating the engagement ring that he intends to give Bathsheba. Finally, **Scene 7**, featuring Troy and Pennyways, leaves us in no doubt that both Bathsheba and Boldwood are in for a shock!

Chapter 53 *Concurritur – Horae Momento*

◆ Boldwood holds his Christmas party.
◆ As Bathsheba plans to leave, Boldwood gets from her a promise to marry him.
◆ Troy appears and claims Bathsheba.
◆ Boldwood shoots Troy and then tries to shoot himself.

The chapter title means "Battle is joined – in a moment of time." See if you think it appropriate. Much of this chapter is concerned with the rustics, the workers of both Bathsheba and Boldwood. They discuss the rumors of Troy's return that have not yet reached their employers. They also discuss their views of the situation, acting as a chorus and putting the dramatic events of the main characters' lives in an everyday context. Laban Tall speaks well of Bathsheba, and one of them comments that *"She never do tell women's little lies."* The rustic chorus also fulfills a warning role. One of them comments: *"More harm may come of this than we know of."*

None of the rustics is quite man enough to break the news to Boldwood or Bathsheba, and so the party goes ahead, though without much real merriment. Boldwood is preoccupied. Just as Bathsheba is about to go, he asks again for a promise of marriage. His stubborn persistence gets the better of Bathsheba in the end. She is *beaten into non-resistance*.

Troy is seen at the window. Note Laban Tall's unintentionally ironic line, *"O no, sir, nobody is dead."* ❷ Who, in particular, is not dead? Troy's entry is high drama. At first – with more irony – Boldwood welcomes him in, failing to recognize him. Troy tries to take Bathsheba away. She screams, and in a moment Troy lies dead, shot at point-blank range by Boldwood, who then tries to shoot himself. ❷ What do you feel about Troy's death? And is Boldwood motivated by hatred or love?

Chapter 54 *After the Shock*

◆ Boldwood walks to Casterbridge and gives himself up.
◆ Bathsheba sends Gabriel for a doctor.
◆ Before the doctor arrives, she lays out Troy's body herself, then faints.

While Boldwood is taking his last walk as a free man, Bathsheba is demonstrating her strength of character.

Even now, she shows herself to be a devoted wife, cradling Troy in her arms and then preparing his body for burial. However, her job done, she demonstrates that *her fortitude had been more of will than of spontaneity*, she faints.

Chapter 55 *The Following March–"Bathsheba Boldwood"*

◆ Boldwood has been sentenced to death, but there may be a reprieve.
◆ Evidence of Boldwood's mental instability is discovered in the clothes and jewelry for "Bathsheba Boldwood" he has kept locked in a closet.
◆ A petition for reconsideration of the sentence is sent to the authorities.
◆ Boldwood's death sentence is changed to life imprisonment.

This is another chapter in which news of events comes to us mostly through the rustics, who have considerable sympathy for Boldwood, especially when it is discovered that he had hoarded presents for Bathsheba in a locked closet: the *somewhat pathetic evidences of a mind crazed with care and love*.

The rustics are also concerned about Bathsheba. Liddy comments on how much she has changed: *"Only two years ago she was a romping girl, and now she's this!"* Liddy is afraid that Bathsheba will suffer more if Boldwood is hanged. Luckily, he is given life imprisonment instead. ✪ How do you imagine Boldwood himself receives the news?

Chapter 56 *Beauty in Loneliness – After All*

◆ Bathsheba visits the grave of Fanny and Troy.
◆ She meets Gabriel, who is going into the church. He reveals his plans to emigrate.
◆ She receives his formal resignation and is desolate.
◆ She goes to see him, thinking she has offended him.
◆ By the end of the chapter, they are to be married.

Like many chapters, this one begins with the season. We learn that Bathsheba has *revived with the spring*. She visits the churchyard and derives satisfaction from viewing what is now the grave of both Fanny and Troy. Presumably it is Bathsheba who has arranged this. ✪ What does this say about her character? She has come a long way emotionally to be able to view the grave the way she does now.

She begins to cry as she hears the children singing. See how the hymn seems to fit her mood and circumstances. Gabriel appears and tells of his plans to emigrate, then leaves her to cope alone with her distress. The year passes, and he becomes increasingly distant. Finally, Bathsheba receives his notice in writing, the day after Christmas, and she is again reduced to bitter tears.

She visits him, and there is a touching scene that is saved from sentimentality by the hint of humor in their awkward exchange over whether Bathsheba said it was *"Too soon"* or *"Too absurd"* to think of marrying him. By the end of the chapter, there is clearly a tender understanding between them, based on a tried-and-tested friendship and *hard prosaic reality*.

❂ Read the final paragraph again. It gives a good summing up of Hardy's attitude toward love and marriage. Try to put it in your own words.

Chapter 57 *A Foggy Night and Morning–Conclusion*

◆ Gabriel arranges a quiet wedding.
◆ The wedding takes place and the couple returns to Bathsheba's house.
◆ They are serenaded and cheered by the rustics.

Although this chapter is unnecessary to the plot, it does round off the book. Gabriel confides in Jan Coggan that he has to get a marriage license, because Bathsheba wants a quiet wedding without any fuss. We hear that Coggan has been *true as steel* during Gabriel's time of unhappiness. Then Bathsheba confides in Liddy, who becomes nervously excited in sympathy with her mistress. It is important that we see Gabriel with a fellow man and Bathsheba with another woman, before the marriage. This reinforcement of manhood and womanhood is somehow necessary before marriage, hence the tradition of "stag" and "hen" nights.

Also very important is the loyal support of the rustics, which marks the marriage's social significance, confers a blessing, and starts the marriage off with a down-to-earth humor that will help to ensure its happiness.

Two more testing tasks!

?   Draw a storyboard showing the key points in the scene at Boldwood's party, from Troy's entry to Boldwood's exit (or write an illustration caption for each frame).

?   How have Gabriel and Bathsheba changed since Chapter 1? Record your observations in the form of a Mind Map, a diagram, or notes.

now that you've reached the end of the Commentary, take a well-earned break

TOPICS FOR DISCUSSION AND BRAINSTORMING

One of the best ways to review is with one or more friends. Even if you're with someone who hardly knows the text you are studying, you'll find that having to explain things to your friend will help you to organize your own thoughts and memorize key points. If you're with someone who has studied the text, you'll find that the things you can't remember are different from the things your friend can't remember so you'll be able to help each other.

Discussion will also help you to develop interesting new ideas that perhaps neither of you would have had alone. Use a brainstorming approach to tackle any of the topics listed below. Allow yourself to share whatever ideas come into your head, however meaningless they seem. They will get you thinking creatively.

Whether alone or with a friend, use Mind Mapping (see p. v) to help you brainstorm and organize your ideas. If you are with a friend, use a large sheet of paper and colored pens.

Any of the topics below could appear on an exam, but even if you think you've found one on your actual exam, be sure to answer the precise question given.

TOPICS

1 Discuss the use of death to usher in new beginnings and plot developments in *Far from the Madding Crowd*.
2 How far has each major character developed by the end of the novel?
3 On the evidence of *Far from the Madding Crowd*, how far do you think Hardy believed in free will?
4 Gabriel is much too good to be true, and Troy much too bad. Discuss.
5 Fanny speaks only a handful of lines. What is her importance as a character?
6 Take an important episode in the novel and consider how you would present it (a) in a film, and (b) on stage.

HOW TO GET AN "A" IN ENGLISH LITERATURE

In all your study, in coursework, and in exams, be aware of the following:

- **Characterization** – the characters and how we know about them (what they say and do, how the author describes them), their relationships, and how they develop.
- **Plot and structure** – what happens and how the plot is organized into parts or episodes.
- **Setting and atmosphere** – the changing scene and how it reflects the story (for example, a rugged landscape and storm reflecting a character's emotional problems).
- **Style and language** – the author's choice of words, and literary devices such as imagery, and how these reflect the mood.
- **Viewpoint** – how the story is told (for example, through an imaginary narrator, or in the third person but through the eyes of one character – "She was furious – how dare he!").
- **Social and historical context** – influences on the author (see Background in this guide).

Develop your ability to:

- Relate **detail** to **broader content, meaning, and style**.
- Show understanding of the author's **intentions, technique, and meaning** (brief and appropriate comparisons with other works by the same author will earn credit).
- Give a **personal response and interpretation**, backed up by **examples** and short **quotations**.
- **Evaluate** the author's achievement (how far does the author succeed and why?).

Make sure you:

- Know how to use **paragraphs** correctly.
- Use a wide range of **vocabulary** and sentence structure.
- Use short appropriate quotations as **evidence** of your understanding of that part of the text.
- Use **literary terms** to show your understanding of what the author is trying to achieve with language.

THE EXAM ESSAY

PLANNING

A literary essay of about 250 to 400 words on a theme from *Far from the Madding Crowd* will challenge your skills as an essay writer. It is worth taking some time to plan your essay carefully. An excellent way to do this is in the three stages below:

1 Make a **Mind Map of** your ideas on the theme suggested. Brainstorm and write down any ideas that pop into your head.
2 Taking ideas from your Mind Map, **organize** them into an outline choosing a logical sequence of information. Choose significant details and quotations to support your main thesis.
3 Be sure you have both a strong **opening paragraph** stating your main idea and giving the title and author of the literary work you will be discussing, and a **conclusion** that sums up your main points.

Then write the essay, allowing five minutes at the end for checking relevance, and spelling, grammar, and punctuation.

Writing and editing

Write your essay carefully, allowing at least five minutes at the end to check for errors of fact as well as for correct spelling, grammar, and punctuation.
REMEMBER!
Stick to the thesis you are trying to support and avoid unnecessary plot summary. Always support your ideas with relevant details and quotations from the text.

Model answer and plan

The next (and final) chapter consists of a model essay on a theme from *Far from the Madding Crowd*, followed by a Mind Map and an essay plan used to write it. Use these to get an idea of how an essay about *Far from the Madding Crowd* might be organized and how to break up your information into a logical sequence of paragraphs.

MODEL ANSWER AND ESSAY PLAN

Before reading the answer, you might like to do a plan of your own, then compare it with the example. The numbered points with comments at the end show why it's a good answer.

QUESTION

Comment on the relationship between major and minor characters in *Far from the Madding Crowd*

PLAN

1 Social and historical context.
2 Literary context.
3 Minor characters comment on major characters and events.
4 Minor characters convey information.
5 Mutual responsibility.
6 Major characters demonstrate their strengths and faults by how they treat the minor ones.
7 Comparison between the major and minor characters.
8 Plot – minor characters as spurs to action.

ESSAY

In *Far from the Madding Crowd* Hardy is writing not just about a handful of individuals, but about a community.[1] It is a traditional rural community, which few people ever move into or leave and in which everyone has a recognized role. We see this in Chapter 10, *Mistress and Men*, as the procession of respectful workers meet their new mistress and recount what they do on the farm and what they get paid for doing it.[2]

Life is hard, and there is a real possibility of winding up in the workhouse (like Fanny) so the mutual responsibility between employers, like Bathsheba and Boldwood, and their employees is all the more important.[3] Gabriel, as a major character who nonetheless is a working man and has the trust of the other men, is in a special position, between Bathsheba and her workers.

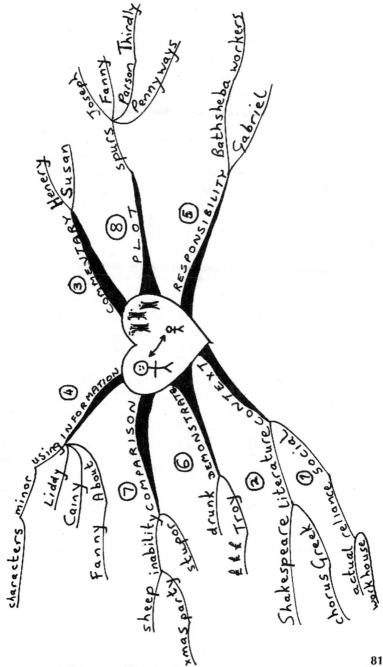

The major–minor relationship is also important in a literary sense. Hardy uses the minor characters, particularly the working men like Jospeph Poorgrass, Jan Coggan, and Mark Clark, as a chorus, as used in Greek tragedy. There are also similarities between Hardy's use of these characters and Shakespeare's use of similar characters (for example the "mechanicals" in *A Midsummer Night's Dream*).[4]

The chorus traditionally comments on events and on the actions of the major characters. In *Far from the Madding Crowd* we see this, for example, in the men's opinions about Bathsheba as a mistress, and on her parents and uncle, given in the chapter set in the malthouse (Chapter 8).[5] There is also Henery Fray's comment on Bathsheba's independence (Chapter 22): "I don't see why a maid should take a husband when she's bold enough to fight her own battles."[6] Another example is when Gabriel starts to do well for himself, and Susan Tall says he's becoming quite a dandy.

Another traditional function of the chorus is their relaying of information about the major characters.[7] This is seen, for example, in William Smallbury's announcement that Fanny has run off with Troy (Chapter 10), and in Cainy Ball's reported sighting of Bathsheba with Troy in Bath (Chapter 33).[8]

We also learn about the major characters by how they treat the minor ones.[9] Gabriel treats the men with fairness and authority. Troy either leads them into bad ways, as when he gets them too drunk to help save the grain from a storm, or patronizes them, as when he throws money to Coggan. Boldwood and Bathsheba show concern and responsibility for Fanny (who is a minor character in terms of her active role, but quite a major one in terms of events that she sets off). In a chance meeting, Gabriel gives her a shilling. Troy seduces and then betrays her.

Major characters also show their strengths and weaknesses in relation to the minor ones. Thus, Gabriel is protecting the grain while the men are in a stupor, and on more than one occasion his efficiency is compared with their confused panic. Bathsheba is a nobler spirit than Liddy, but we see her behave badly when her temper almost makes Liddy leave. We also see that Bathsheba has a frivolous side to her, which is quite like Liddy, when she sends the valentine. On the language level, the rustics often make fools of themselves (for example by using "persecute" for "prosecute," or in drunken philosophizing), whereas the major characters don't.[10]

Finally, the minor characters act as spurs to the plot. Their deeds, or misdeeds, often have important effects on the major characters. The prime example is when Joseph fails to deliver Fanny's coffin. This results in the dramatic scene in which Troy kisses Fanny's corpse and then leaves Weatherbury.

To conclude, the story of Hardy's novel is about the main characters, but it is always placed in context by the minor ones.[11]

WHAT'S SO GOOD ABOUT IT?

1 Strong opening sentence makes a statement on which the rest of the essay stands.
2 Good examples are used for making point about social context.
3 General point ties in social and historical context with exact essay title.
4 Shows awareness of literary context.
5 Good example of Hardy's use of rustics as chorus.
6 Good use of a quotation.
7 Moves on neatly to next point.
8 Good use of evidence.
9 Perceptive comment on Hardy's characterization.
10 Shows awareness of language.
11 Neat, concise conclusion.

GLOSSARY OF LITERARY TERMS

alliteration repetition of a sound at the beginnings of words, such as *ladies' lips.*

context the social and historical influences on the author.

foreshadowing an indirect warning of things to come, often through imagery.

image a word picture used to make an idea come alive; for example, a **metaphor**, **simile**, or **personification** (see separate entries).

imagery the kind of word picture used to make an idea come alive.

irony (1) where the author or a character says the opposite of what they really think, or pretends ignorance of the true facts, usually for the sake of humor or ridicule; (2) where events turn out in what seems a particularly inappropriate way, as if mocking human effort.

metaphor a description of a thing as if it were something essentially different, but also in some way similar; for example, *the sun bristled down* (Chapter 47).

personification a description of something (such as fate) as if it were a person.

setting the place in which the action occurs, usually affecting the atmosphere, such as the malthouse or the seaside.

simile a comparison of two things that are different in most ways but similar in one important way; for example, the sea *which licked the ... stones like tongues* (Chapter 47).

structure how the plot is organized.

theme an idea explored by an author; for example, time and change.

viewpoint how the story is told; for example, through action, or in discussion between minor characters.

INDEX

Page references in bold denote major character or theme sections.

architecture 23, 34, 44, 67
army 2, 35
atmosphere 20, 27, 36, 56, 61, 78
Bathsheba Everdene **11–13**
  grief 63–64, 69
  independence 11, 12–13, 19, 34, 39, 49, 60, 82
  love 50
  pride 12, 43, 65
  skills 23, 41
  unpredictability 12, 23, 37–38, 50
  vanity 26, 37
  virtues 12, 19, 28, 60, 62, 63
Boldwood, Farmer **10–11**
  despair 11, 54, 55
  hopes 70, 73
  naivety 10
  obsession 10, 11, 17, 18, 41, 52, 57, 75
  persistence 11, 39, 71
  protector 19, 69, 74
  responsibility 10
  seriousness 38, 41, 42
Christmas party 73–74
Clark, Mark 61
Coggan, Jan 14, 18, 52–53, 61, 76
context 1–2, 78
craft 23, 34, 43–44, 67
  see also under individual characters
Fanny Robin 13, 19, 33, 35, 40, 59, 60, 82
fate 22–3, 31, 37–8, 41, 44, 58, 62, 65, 67–68, 69
foreshadowing 46, 48, 53
Fray, Henery 14, 34
Hardy, Thomas, life of 1
harvest supper 55
imagery 26, 30, 32, 36, 38–39, 52, 57, 65, 69, 78
irony 14, 59, 73, 74
Liddy 13, 18, 19, 34, 37, 50, 62, 82
love **16–18**
  aspects 16–17
  destructive 52, 57, 63
  falling in 29, 41, 42, 46
  folly 17, 29, 41, 42, 56
  goddess of 16, 32, 45
  romantic 17–18, 28, 39, 60
  sexual 37, 46, 49
  songs 45
loyalty **18**
  Coggan's 76
  Gabriel's 7, 29, 39, 56
  lack of 18, 59
  rustics' 76

men and women **18–20**
  attitudes 19, 36, 43, 47, 52
  marriage 19, 43, 76
  qualities (female) 28, 32, 34–35, 37, 57, 64, 68, 74; (male) 34
  sexuality 49
  worlds 34, 37, 38
names (of characters) 7, 10, 48
nature **20–21**
  descriptions 20, 27, 42, 61, 65, 68–69
  goddess of 64
  knowledge of 21, 32, 55–56
  power 32, 56, 57
  seasons 20–1, 36, 41, 42, 44, 70, 75
  symbolism 49
Oak, Gabriel **6–8**
  appearance 26
  books 33
  courage 32, 56, 63
  imagination 7, 21, 27–28
  loyalty 7, 18
  naivety 7
  protector 19, 30, 50, 62
  responsibility 62, 82
  skills 6–7, 21, 23, 27, 32, 33, 41, 42, 43, 52–53, 56
Pennyways 1, 32, 33, 71, 73
Poorgrass, Joseph 1, 14, 61
poverty 2, 80
red, color 17, 26, 47, 65
religion 2, 22
rick fire 32
rustics 14, 33, 70, 73, 76, 80–83
setting 20–21, 61, 78
sexes *see* men and women
shearing-supper 45
storm 55–56
Tall, Laban 14, 74
time **21–22**
  age 22, 44, 54
  change 29, 32, 42, 70, 75
  moment 21–22, 27, 40, 47
  seasons 20–21, 36, 44, 70, 75
Troy, Sergeant Francis **8–10**
  cruelty 54, 58
  death 74
  disloyalty 8, 18
  irresponsibility 9, 21, 23, 48, 55, 56, 58, 82
  romanticism 17–18, 63–66
  sex-appeal 8–9, 20
  skills 9, 23, 49, 71
  time, sense of 21–22, 40, 48
  unpredictability 8, 48, 56–57
valentine 17, 37–38